The
Feathered
Cloak

The Feathered Cloak

THE TRILOGY OF THE TREE
PART I

SEAN DIXON

KEY PORTER BOOKS

Library and Archives Canada Cataloguing in Publication

Dixon, Sean
The feathered cloak / Sean Dixon.

ISBN-13: 978-1-55263-936-8, ISBN-10: 1-55263-936-3

I. Title.

PS8557.I97F43 2007   jC813'.54   C2007-902114-X

THE CANADA COUNCIL | LE CONSEIL DES ARTS
FOR THE ARTS | DU CANADA
SINCE 1957 | DEPUIS 1957

ONTARIO ARTS COUNCIL
CONSEIL DES ARTS DE L'ONTARIO

The publisher gratefully acknowledges the support of the Canada Council for the Arts and the Ontario Arts Council for its publishing program. We acknowledge the support of the Government of Ontario through the Ontario Media Development Corporation's Ontario Book Initiative.

We acknowledge the financial support of the Government of Canada through the Book Publishing Industry Development Program (BPIDP) for our publishing activities.

Key Porter Books Limited
Six Adelaide Street East, Tenth Floor
Toronto, Ontario
Canada M5C 1H6

www.keyporter.com

Illustrations: Brian Deines

Text design: Martin Gould

Printed and bound in Canada

07 08 09 10 11 5 4 3 2 1

This book is for Kat
and in memory of Wendy Shook

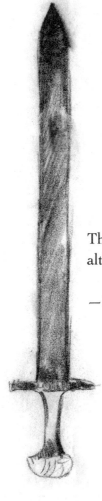

The outcome is in the balance,
although the fight takes place in the air.

— Pliny the Elder

Freya in Her Forest

THIS IS THE STORY of an ambitious and bad-tempered young girl named Freya, who lived outside of Trondheim in the northern part of Norway more than a thousand years ago. I will do my best to explain to you why she was generally so cross and rude, so that you might sympathize with her a little and perhaps accept her as the true, stout-hearted subject of my tale instead of snapping this book shut and heading off to seek out the company of more pleasant heroes in more pleasant books.

Freya was the daughter of a peasant, a goatherd, who tended a field at the edge of a forest. All her life she had lived between that forest and that field, in a house with a red painted door. All her life she had played in that forest with her little brother Rolf. For many years, the two of them had been so small that they would sit together quietly underneath a bush, almost invisible, while the animals of the forest went about their business all around them. It was a time of magic in Freya's memory, when anything seemed possible, all within the grasp of a girl who might simply reach out to touch and understand as creatures passed by and paid her no heed.

Unusual among the fair people of the North, Freya had black hair and black eyes and skin as dark as any Persian's. She stood out even darker beside her pale, red-headed brother, who looked more like a typical child of a typical Norseman. Children in the village had always mocked Freya for what they saw as her dirty-face looks, but she didn't mind. With her father and her brother, she had made a world at the edge of that wood and no one could trouble her in it.

For a long time, the sun had shone brightly down upon the forest, through the pines, making the forest floor a dappled place of light and shade. As Freya grew, she came to love these spots of light and darkness more than anything else in the world. In the light, she saw birds and butterflies and spinning spiders hanging from sunny threads. In the shadows, she saw creatures big and small that kept their distance, travelling in the realm just beyond the clear end of her vision—a realm that is most beautiful of all, since it beckons you to come and see it, and see yet another distance again stretching off farther than you can see. The earth is big and nothing is more beautiful to a child than distance; is this not true? I am a very old man; perhaps I do not remember correctly.

But I stray from my story. I was speaking of the creatures that seemed to always keep their distance from Freya's eye as they moved through the faraway of the forest, returning from their journeys only in the depths of night to come closer in her dreams, travelling past again, turning their heads to look at her with majestic antlers and bright green eyes, fearful and wonderful.

And Freya pretended to travel through the farthest reaches of the forest, though truly she never strayed far from the edge with its fields and farmhouse and goats, with her father and brother to bring her home and make her human again when she had spent a whole day imagining herself a fox or a hare. Sometimes she would crawl in the shadows and pretend to be a strange kind of hunter, with flashing eyes and wings curled at her shoulders, ready at a moment's notice to spring into flight. This desire for flight overtook her so strongly sometimes that she would spend obsessive hours hurling pinecones toward the tops of trees, imagining that they were her own body slipping the bonds of gravity. But even these pinecones, small as they were, seamed with pockets of air, came spinning back to the ground.

Sometimes in the forest, she thought she saw the kind of hunter she pretended to be, two of them in fact, far away in the trees: two women on horseback who always travelled from the West, always toward the North. They were noble in stature, riding high on their dark horses and close to one another, faces forward and fixed. Though it may have only been a trick of the distant light and shade, they each seemed to have an enormous pair of wings folded over their backs. Freya saw them so rarely, however, that sometimes she thought she had never seen them at all, and had only pretended, had only dreamt them up.

And her father fed her imagination too, collecting stones and bones from his goatherd wanderings, and bringing them back to her with elaborate explanations about their origins—some farfetched, others seeming true, still others with many meanings that could only be guessed. He had once brought home a little amber stone, which he told her was one of the tears of the goddess Freya.

"Whenever the goddess cries," he said, "she sheds tears of gold, and when those tears fall upon the trees of the earth, they turn to amber as they roll down the trunks."

"That's my name," said Freya.

"That's true," her father replied. "But it is also the name of a goddess: the most beautiful, and one of the most powerful."

"I was named after a goddess?" asked Freya.

"That's right," said her father.

"Who named me?"

"I named you."

"And why did you name me after a goddess?"

"Because it was a pretty name."

"So nobody else helped to name me?"

"Nobody else."

Perhaps I should mention here that there was an unspoken understanding between Freya and her father, going back almost as far as she could remember, that they would never utter the word "mother." She had experimented once, while looking at her own reflection in a mirror. Behind her, in the glass, she saw her father's face fall so far that she feared he might never raise it. So she never spoke the word again. Still, every question she asked in those days had that word (mother) curled up inside it like a secret paper in a wish, or sometimes like a bee hidden inside a flower, depending on her mood.

He was such a good and loving man, her father, and he gave both her and Rolf their own little rooms in the small house with the red painted door they all shared between the field and the forest—rooms the size of closets with walls that did not quite reach the ceiling, but rooms nonetheless. There was no reason for Freya to be anything but happy. And she was. She was happy, and she dreamt, and she grew.

But in her eleventh year many things began to change. Everything that was fine and fair and warm and small in her life began to disappear and be replaced by things that were stupid and ugly, cold and big, and more than a little scary. For one thing—the main thing really—her little brother Rolf turned into a big giant oaf. Though he was only nine years old, he suddenly started to grow and grow. He didn't stop growing until he was over ten feet tall. No longer could they sit silently together under a bush and let the animals of the forest go about their business. In fact, most of the bushes they used to sit under had been trampled by the oafish, clumsy, stupid, inconsiderate colossus of a Rolf. And there were no longer dapples of light and shadow in the forest: The sky had been cloudy and grey for every single day of the last year! And then the snow came falling down and never left! Rolf could walk around in it without any difficulty, the big, stupid, red-headed oaf. In fact, he was always striding to and fro in the snow without really having anywhere to go. Freya, for her part, was still small for her age and often sank into drifts up to her waist. She had to learn how to walk with large, clumsy snowshoes.

If all this weren't enough, their father had begun to grow gloomy, bleary-eyed, and wandery.

In better days, he had often told her the story of a time before she remembered when he had come home smarting about some social slight he had endured in the village, when he'd been mocked or snubbed by someone or other. Freya, no more than three years old, had looked at him as he grumbled and she had jumped up and shouted, "Those people know nothing!"

And he, taken aback, had replied, "How can you

prove that, Freya, my daughter?"

"Because they prefer cows' milk to goats'!"

Just like that, out of the blue from his three-year-old daughter. He had laughed and laughed, and his laughter was infectious, so that first Freya was caught up in it, and then later, as the story got told again and again, the young tiny Rolf, until the sound of all their laughter rang through the field and the forest and reached as far as Trondheim where, for reasons they could not have cared less about, they seemed to have no friends.

"That's why I love you, my daughter," her father had told her then, and again and again. "You make me understand very well that I have no need of anyone but you and your brother!"

But now it was hard to believe he had ever said such things. He sank further and further into the gloom, even as the green fields crawled farther and farther beneath their blankets of snow. Sometimes he would look distracted and make strange boasts about things she had never heard before and did not like: how his family line could be traced all the way back to Odin himself, father of all the gods, or that he'd once been a king, or a traveller of faraway places, in a time of the world that was lost. If he had told her such stories with pride and with love, they might have enriched her wonder, her curiosity and imagination, but these were bitter boasts that brought him no pleasure and her no understanding. He blurted them out and never explained.

Most frightening of all was when he told how once he had witnessed a battle the likes of which no one had ever seen—a battle that had changed the world—and that he had lost everything he'd ever loved in it. And then he would pause and add, almost reluctantly, "Except for you, of course. Except for both of you."

Freya would ask, "What battle? What battle do you mean?" But he would sigh and speak no more. And so Freya came to think her father must have needed something other than her and her brother, and that this long-standing need had begun to cling to him and wear on him, as the snow clung to and wore the earth. And she wished she knew what it was and where it was and whether it was really lost in some unknown battle. She cried now when she thought of that story, and when she touched her face with her fingers, she felt tears that were not made of gold at all, but rather just water.

And her tears exhausted her so much that she found she did not mind when her father wandered further afield through the days, searching for new places for his goats to graze. She realized that she preferred to be cross and angry all the time than to be sad, which is what she felt these days when she looked at her silent father and saw how different he had become. He spent so little time with his children and so much time with his goats that Freya thought he was beginning to look himself like a wild animal. Not so much a goat as an old, tired, wild boar.

I imagine you're wondering why I can't devise some

kind of contrivance to get my heroine out of this landscape of gloom and sadness, really, this very frightening
place. A contraption for flying, perhaps? By which she
might fly a thousand miles in a minute or two? To the
newly reorganized library of Alexandria and take out a
book, perhaps? Or over the civilized cities of Arabia, to
alight at the shoulder of the learned Ibn Isa as he puts the
finishing touches on his new masterpiece of calligraphy?

Or perhaps I could contrive to give Freya a chair
that travels through time and then she could jump to
the future and come and visit you? And then perhaps
she could tell you her own story in her own way and I
could just shuffle off to bed and get a good night's sleep
for a change.

Alas, I cannot allow any of this to happen, since I
am not in control of the matter. This is a true story, and
it begins right here in this bleak northern landscape, in
this northern part of Norway, just outside of
Trondheim, between this forest and this field.

So this is how we find Freya: always alone in the forest,
always lonely. She wanted nothing more than to leave
this sad, grey land and go to some sunny, warm country.
As her snowshoes thudded over the dull terrain, she
imagined a country where the colour grey had been
banished altogether by royal decree. As she perched
pointlessly on the branches of a lifeless tree, she

dreamt of a land where leaves were so thick and big and green that she could pluck one for a sturdy boat and another for a sail; and then she would travel to still more distant lands, where she would become a great and learned scholar-warrior-queen. Such were the dreams the unhappy Freya dreamt as she wandered alone through the sullen forest.

Recently, however, she had stopped dreaming dreams and started planning plans. Everything had changed, you see, on the day that Freya saw the strange little man in the forest.

The Servant of the King

ONE DAY, FREYA was out walking and dreaming and dreaming and walking, as was her usual habit, when suddenly, just ahead, she saw a crude little hut made of sticks and sap and string. It was very strange, it looked like it had been there for a long time, and Freya wondered why she had never seen it before. Then she saw the little man huddled inside. He was in shadow, so she could barely make him out, but he had a very long nose that poked from the shadow and gave him away. He must not have been quite aware, it seemed to Freya, of how long his nose was, otherwise he would have kept it hidden with the rest of him in the darkness of the hut. Vanity can give us away in the strangest circumstances. The nose, she observed, hovered there very still, and then she noticed there was a gnarled little fist, just below the nose, poking out of the shadow as well. Clutched in the fist was the end of a piece of twine that trailed away into a small clearing.

Freya had stopped and now stood very still. Never before had she seen such a stranger in her forest. She felt a sudden flush of bad temper. Really, it was just too much. What right did this man have to build a hut and clutch a piece of twine in her forest? Inside her head she was shouting rude remarks, but her mouth, held in the grip of curiosity, stayed shut tight. Beside her there happened to be a single small bush that had been left miraculously untrampled by her oafish brother. Since Freya was still rather small, somewhat smaller than your average eleven-year-old, she took two quick steps sideways and ducked behind the bush. And then she sat very still, more still even than the nose that poked from the shadow of the hut.

And so things remained for a very long time. The nose in the air did not hover or sniff. The gnarled fist did not yank at its twine. Freya did not budge from behind her untrampled bush. And then, as if it had only just appeared, Freya saw the pigeon. It was poking around in a padded down circle of snow in the centre of the clearing. There was a length of twine tied around its waist. Freya closed one eye, squinted with the other, and followed the trail the length of twine traced all the way to the hut and into the gnarled fist of the man in the shadows with the long and narrow nose. Freya wondered to herself what business a man with a long, narrow nose and gnarled hands had sitting all day very still in the doorway of a small hut, clutching one end of a long length of twine whose other end was tied to a pigeon. It was all too strange and very stupid. She decided that the clutching of a length of twine tied to a pigeon was very likely the most foolish occupation she had ever had the displeasure to witness.

Then the nose moved. Freya saw it move. A moment before it had been level with the ground. Now she saw that it was pointing upwards toward the sky. Freya looked up toward the sky, too.

Just above the trees, Freya saw an enormous falcon. It swooped high up into the sky and then arced down, very close to the tops of the trees and then circled and swooped high again. Although the sky was grey with clouds, the falcon seemed itself to be composed of light and shade. All on its own. Its feathers a shimmering boast that flight can carry a beast above the clouds and into the brightness of a higher world. Some of its feathers were as black as she had ever seen, but among them flashed lines of brilliant white. Such a bird, she realized, could fly so high as to reach above the clouds and see the sun, and carry its rays down to the earth on great and powerful wings.

Swooping high again, the falcon hovered and then suddenly dived. Down it came with incredible speed. It dove past the tops of the trees and down into the clearing. It dove straight for the little pigeon pecking in its small circle of snow. Freya thought that nothing could move as swiftly as this falcon, that nothing could prevent it from scooping up the poor little pigeon, but then something did. The pigeon was gone. Just as the falcon was about to snatch it up, something had yanked it out of the way. Freya looked over at the little hut just in time to see a second gnarled fist appear suddenly beside the first and yank at a second length of twine, which had suddenly appeared, causing a net to fall down from everywhere in the trees above the clearing and enclose the falcon within it.

The long, narrow nose now disappeared from the doorway and was replaced by the emerging face of a grizzled old man. Moving somewhat like a bird himself, the old man hopped from the doorway with a burlap sack in one fist and a cage in the other. In barely a moment of swift efficiency, he rustled the falcon out of the net and into the sack, popped the pigeon into the cage, coiled the two lengths of twine around his arm, and kicked apart his little hut. Suddenly, everything was again as it had been in the forest, except where the snow had been padded down. The old man was clearly skilled at erasing all signs of his business, though he could not hide the fact that he'd been there. Now he held up the sack that contained his captive falcon and poked at it once with his nose. The bag was very still. The man spoke in a high, reedy sort of voice:

"Happy for you the king is fond of falcons. Happy for me. You shall be the finest hunting falcon in the land.

I will train you, I will take you to the king, and I will bend my knee and raise you on my gloved wrist. And then you and I will become honoured servants of Erik, Great King of Norway."

From behind her untrampled bush, Freya had forgotten her bad-temperedness for the moment, and was mouthing the words, "Erik, Great King of Norway; fond of falcons."

Then, just as swiftly as Freya had seen him bag the bird, the old man was gone, disappeared through the trees into the grey afternoon. Freya clumped in her snowshoes over to the place where he had been. She studied the branches of the trees where he had tied his net. She studied the ground where he had run his twine. She studied the marks in the snow to see how everything had happened. Here was the place where the pigeon was pulled. Here were the marks where the falcon had closed its talons over snow, missing the pigeon. And here were the prints of the old man's boots, sunk tidily into snow. It seemed to her that he had not budged from his squatting position for as long as he had been there, waiting patiently to capture a falcon. Around the two sunken footprints lay a few breadcrumbs, some carrot tops and a single chicken bone picked clean.

That was the day when Freya stopped dreaming dreams and started planning plans. She stood in the clearing and made her decision. She was going to become a falcon-catcher. She was going to catch a great and powerful falcon, feathers full of light and shade. She was going to march with her falcon all the way south to the longhouse of the king, for the king was fond of falcons. She was going to bend her knee before the king and raise her falcon upon her gloved wrist and offer it as a gift. In this way, she was going to become an honoured servant of Erik, Great King of Norway. As servant of the king she would travel to distant lands where the sun shone bright and the leaves were green and the colour grey was banished by decree. She would sit at tables with kings and queens and khans and emperors. And they would call her Freya the Small, Freya the Bold, Freya of Norway, Freya the Falcon-Catcher.

The King

BUT ERIK WAS a different sort of king than Freya supposed. His full name was Erik Blood-Axe—if that tells you anything—and he was no friend to faraway kings or queens or khans or emperors, but rather the solitary ruler of the bald and wintry country of Norway.

King Erik was in fact a true Viking, from that legendary tribe of Norsemen who fought many bloody wars, related many tall tales, kept superb family trees, and disappeared from the world, gone long ago to sit forever at the feasting tables of Valhalla, where they regale one another with stories of battle, and where they drink from cups beaten out of copper and bronze, all through eternity.

But in the old days they were really human, walking

in the world, and they contended with real human problems, both out in the world and within their own hearts. It troubled Erik Blood-Axe to hear the old people of his time sigh and pray and say that his country had once been a mild and green and temperate place, because to Erik it was right and just and good that the Norse skies should always be filled with clouds and the Norse forests should always be cloaked in mist, a haven for rooks and owls and hawks and wolves—all of it a fitting environment, he felt, between gritted teeth, for a Viking.

And the Norse earth should always be covered with snow. As indeed it was. There was so much snow, in fact, that all the animals and birds in the countryside had learned to live their daily lives in the snow. No birds flew south and no animals hibernated in the wintertime. They had learned to make the snow their hardscrabble home. Even certain plants had managed to survive, pushing spidery roots deep down into the earth, and poking tender shoots of green up through the white cloak that lay over the land. Moles and rabbits dug tunnels down along the pathways of these roots, and sparrows darted up and about among the snow like angels untouched by its frozen grip. They lived at the very edge of starvation, but they lived. Squirrels whispered to one another about the meaning of such a long winter and filled the hours bundled in their dreys arguing their various opinions and interpretations in the matter—some argued that it foretold peace, others war. It's a little-known fact, you see, that squirrels are meticulous and thorough historians. They keep excellent records and practise their powers of memory by giving their children twenty-syllable names.

But more of that in a later story (or, I should say, a later book). For now it need only be said that some people (and squirrels) went so far as to believe there was a connection between the ascension of Erik and the freezing of Norway. But they must have thought they were living in a fairy tale. The weather is the weather, connected to the ways and workings of the gods — not men. Still, it was, I admit, quite a coincidence, since Erik Blood-Axe was a cruel king whose heart had grown as cold as the snow and no tender shoots sprang forth from it.

King Erik had three hunting falcons in his keep. They mostly sat very still on perches made of gold, with lushly jewelled black hoods covering their eyes. Such is the custom of the falcon-keeper for keeping the falcon at rest: with his eyes covered in this way, a falcon always thinks he is sitting in the dark of night, and instinct forbids such a bird from ever wishing to take flight after the sun has gone down. The wild falcon of the forest sits still through the dark hours on his branch and leaves the night's hunting to his nocturnal cousin the owl. The hooded falcon of the hall sits still on his perch, dreaming of these same bright-eyed cousin-owls swooping through the wood, and patiently waits for the dawn that only comes when the gloved falconer slips the hood up and off his head and away.

Two of Erik's falcons were sleek and young and fast, and dreamt on their perches steadily and constantly of the hunt. The third was very old. He had served for many years as a loyal hunter for the king who had been Erik's father, a man who it was said had begun his reign in a time of greenery and had been hardly bad at all, at least compared to his son. At the time in which our story is being told, the old king had been dead for a year, gone to sit and feast at the tables of Valhalla with his friends and ancestors. The old falcon now served as a hunter for King Erik, though in the service of a cruel man a loyal old servant grows older by the day, and wills himself steadily toward death.

So old had this falcon become, in fact, that some of the human servants in the royal longhouse suspected that he had become wise. They said you would be able see the intelligence in his eyes if only you snuck up and dared to raise the hood, and perceive how he turned his haughty head to look at you. Some of the servants even whispered that this old falcon was no longer fooled by the hood at all. They whispered that he had some-how grasped in a subtle refinement of his memory how beyond this hood of jewelled black—a cloak that served not only to cover his eyes but his wings as well, and so the very desire for flight—there shone the brilliant light of day. The servants spoke over their counters and their candles and in their bedcovers of a time when this old bird had been young, when it was certain how he had loved the sun and been inspired by it: in the wide blue sky of his younger days, he would swoop and dive like no other bird in the land. These days, of course, there was little sun to see, so perhaps it was no matter, they thought, that his old eyes were so constantly shuttered. And since he was so old, they whispered too that he could no longer hunt or fly well. This was a very sad prospect indeed, since a falcon that cannot hunt is of no use at all to the king that joys in killing.

But that's enough of that. Here I am just starting my story and already the candle is ebbing and it is well past my bedtime. Still, there's nothing to be done. I must go on.

Falcon's Fall

ONE DAY a messenger arrived at the main hall
of the longhouse of the king of all Norway
just as Erik was setting out for his morning
hunt. The messenger had, in fact, travelled swiftly through
the whole of the night in the hopes that he would get
himself presented in the time between the moment when
the king first cracked his eggs and the moment of his
breakfast's end, well-known to be the least perilous time
of the day. But, alas, it was not to be. So Erik made the
messenger trudge with him out into the fields beyond
the longhouse, accompanied by his four servants, their
horses, and the three hooded falcons. The morning was
cold and dismal as usual, quite suitable to Erik, and a
heavy mist lay over the snow-covered land. There was
a single long, low hill in the clearing, covered with

bushes that concealed various wildfowl the colour of mud and straw. A copse of trees stood to the east of them, which thickened to a forest in the north that went on for miles.

The horses stood back from the party, snorting in the cold, attended by a single despondent groom—a sullen and self-involved young lad who hadn't even bothered to fill his pockets with oats for the horses, who was, in fact, fated to spend the entire expedition to follow (famous though it was to become in lore legend story and song) fretting obsessively in his mind about the way in which a girl from the kitchen had turned up her nose at him as she gathered kindling several days before.

The messenger stood and waited knee-deep in snow while the king removed the hood from his first falcon and hurled it flapping into the field. This one swooped and stooped and flew back from the other side of the low hill with a grouse clutched in his claws. Erik was well pleased, and held the wriggling grouse aloft in his gauntleted hand. The horses snorted. His four servants emitted a burst of hand flapping and applause, soon followed by an approving bleat from the exhausted messenger, who hoped and dreaded that his time to speak had finally come.

But the time to speak had not yet come and still the messenger had to wait, knee-deep in snow, while King Erik removed the hood from his second falcon. This one flew out into the field and brought back a pheasant from the other side of the low hill. Again the servants and the messenger applauded. Again the horses snorted. Still the groom stood listlessly, bitterly contemplating the tip of the kitchen-girl's nose. Ah well; the poor groom. Perhaps it was just as well. Perhaps he was lucky to be ignored by King Erik Blood-Axe of Norway on this morning, as he stood wearily among the horses, contemplating poetry and a nose.

Weariness hung among all the servants in fact, though the messenger stood weariest of them all, and he observed again that his waiting had not yet come to an end. The king was now removing the hood from his third falcon, his old and loyal falcon; the falcon that had served his father before him. He hurled this one flapping out into the field as he had the two lithe and youthful falcons before it.

When King Erik observed, however, that this third falcon was not swift to return from the other side of the low hill, he began to grow impatient. Aside from being a man of certain set routines, Erik was also well-known to be an impatient man. It's a terrible combination of qualities in a king, and in anyone else for that matter. Erik, truth be told, was somewhat ashamed of his capacity for impatience, which he felt, accurately as it turns out, to be a weakness in his character; but shame never prevented him from indulging his impatience to the full extent of its capacity. Now, as he watched his loyal falcon hop about in the snow at the top of the hill, unable to catch even the slowest pheasant, swooping and stooping in a particularly barren spot as if it were teeming with prey, Erik grew ever more and more impatient. He grew so impatient, in fact, that he began to wonder about the messenger and his message. Or perhaps it's more accurate to say that he skipped wondering altogether and zeroed straight in on irritable speculation, annoyance, and aggravation. This only made things worse of course, since he felt that if he were to demand that the messenger deliver his message before the third falcon had completed its task, then he would certainly prove among his retinue to be an impatient king, a king who did not do things properly and in order, a king in fact who conducted his affairs in a flagrantly, shamefully impatient manner. Still, he couldn't help himself. He began to observe the messenger with one eye and his old failing falcon with the other. Finally, he could not stand it anymore: his eyes crossed, he farted with annoyance, a cloud of steam shot from his nostrils, and he commanded the messenger to speak.

"I bring news of your brother Haakon," said the messenger, in a somewhat tremulous voice.

Oh yes, I forgot. Turns out I have to go back and set some scenes, it seems. Sigh. The old king, Erik's father, whose name was Harald, actually had two sons: Erik and Haakon. King Harald kept the elder son, Erik, for himself and sent the infant son, Haakon, to England to be raised by the English King Athelston. Harald did this, believe it or not, on account of the fact that he was jealous of Athelston's reputation as a great and honourable warrior and a good man to boot. He knew that although he himself would be content to neglect his own son, the good King Athelston would not. Still further, he knew that Athelston would never refuse such a request to take the infant Haakon into his charge, and so he packed his son off to England for the simple reason that he knew that the honourable Athelston would take charge of the baby, that he would feed it and care for it and dote on it and raise it, and that finally the distraction of a newly beloved child would weaken the English king, and turn him aside from his warrior ways, leaving the world at the feet of the Viking Harald to conquer. This is the way in which the affairs of state were conducted in those days.

And so it came to pass. Harald left Erik to be raised by servants while he himself planned campaigns and led armies into battle. Athelston, over in England, gradually gave up his warrior's life and doted more and more on Haakon, his adopted son. Harald became known as the greatest warrior in all of Europe, while Athelston grew old and weak and, some said, wise. Certainly he came to love his life. And their sons grew too. To put it in the starkest and simplest possible terms, it seems that Haakon grew to be more and more good, while Erik grew to be more and more evil. Haakon grew up to be a lissome and willowy young man, and Erik grew up to be the grizzled, ambitious, and impatient king of Norway. Haakon learned the ways of justice and compassion from his adopted father, while Erik learned from his own father nothing but the wish and the will for power.

That should be enough about Haakon to keep you going. I am, after all, on my second candle, and though it's true I have collected the wax to be reused, wicks themselves are troublesome to come by these days, and rather too expensive, if you ask me.

"I bring news of your brother Haakon," said the messenger.

King Erik watched as in the middle distance his old falcon tumbled silently through the snow of the low hilltop. "My baby brother Haakon," he said, since he felt compelled to correct people even when there was no need.

"I bring news of your baby brother Haakon," said the messenger and trembled a little.

King Erik watched as his old falcon snagged his left claw on a root that protruded from the snow and then somersaulted, unbelievably, four times through the air, landing headfirst in a bank. It took several minutes for the bird to dislodge itself, and the king watched, half hoping the creature would give up and lie still, but it did not.

"What news of my baby brother Haakon," said King Erik, finally. It should have been a question, but it was not, and this flummoxed the messenger a little, who realized there was no obstacle left toward the delivery of his news. He swiftly decided to hesitate.

"The Tronds of Trondheim," he said. "I also bring news of them. The Tronds of Trondheim and also your baby brother Haakon, all at the same time. I bring news of all of them, er, together."

"Then tell me," said Erik, relishing this opportunity for a semblance of patience, "what could it be that my baby brother, who lives well and safely back from the far cliffs of England, could possibly have in common with the Tronds of Trondheim, Norway."

"I bring news that, er, the news is brought by me that, er, facts really, that would not change one bit whether I, the messenger, were to bring news of them or not. Facts have been established that point to the truth of the fact of the matter, and so news must be brought, loyally and, er, courageously and succinctly, that ..."

The messenger was still groping for the words. The falcon was still struggling headfirst in the snow.

"Finish it," said Erik, whose eyes had nearly crossed for a second time.

"... that the Tronds of Trondheim have made your brother their king."

Steam came forth from Erik's nose, and also, if the attending servants were to be believed later on in the longhouse kitchen, his ears.

"That's odd," said the king, still patiently. "Trondheim is a part of Norway, is it not? Or is this another Trondheim of which you speak? A Trondheim of Denmark or England, or perhaps even a Trondheim in the region of Constantinople? Perhaps there is a Trondheim in one of the countries of the southern Slavs, or perhaps even in the steppes of the northern Slavs? Seems unlikely to me though: the only Trondheim I am the least bit aware of is a minor region of Norway, right here, in the middle-northern part of my own country, on the coast, where you can look across and wave delicately, if you wish, toward the distant shores of Iceland."

This last word, Iceland, he said as if it had four syllables.

"The only Trondheim of which I am aware," he added, "is Trondheim, Norway. And I am king of all of Norway, am I not?"

Everyone stood silently for a long time. So long they stood, in fact, that on the seeming other side of the world in a small monastery in Ireland, a young monk began and completed some decidedly masterful brush-work of the letter "C" in the title of an illuminated manuscript of the *Consolation of Philosophy*. True, too, that during this silence, across the ocean beyond the monk's window, in the land now known as North America, after negotiations that had gone late into the night, five hands were clasped that first brought five tribes together into the Iroquois Confederacy, a bond that would not be broken for a thousand years and more. And then, at last, unbeknownst to the monk sitting quietly at his table and the five Iroquois chiefs sitting by their fire, the Norse King Erik of the Northern European country of Norway spoke again.

"Look at that sad excuse for a bird of prey."

The messenger mustered what little courage he had left, after running all through the night and trembling all through the morning.

"Haakon arrived last week from England, and, and, the Tronds immediately, immediately crowned him. He says that . . . he says he will give the land back to the people who live on it. He says he does not wish to plan wars or, or, or, campaigns. That is a direct . . . quote. He spends his days sk — . . . he spends his days sk — . . ."

The messenger took a deep breath.

"He spends his days skiing through the snow-gilded forests of, of, Trondheim, planning how to make the country just and, just and, safe."

King Erik turned and fixed his gaze briefly on the messenger before turning back to the seeming death-throes of his oldest and most useless falcon.

"Skiing," he said.

"Sk-iing, yes, your . . . your . . . your . . ."

The messenger couldn't remember whether he was to say "Majesty" or "Highness" or "Bloodiness" or "Sharpness" or "Axeness" or what.

"Skiing," said King Erik again. "What is this 'skiing'?"

"He w — he wears flat sticks upon his feet and with their aid slides along on the top of the snow."

"How absurd," groused the King. "How ridiculous. A man with sliding feet. He must look as ridiculous as that old bird yonder, skidding desperately through the snow."

The messenger spoke again, pulling up the last little condensations of courage and loyalty from the deep dry well inside him. "They call him Haakon the Good," he said. "I have heard . . . I have heard . . ."

He started again.

"I have heard some people say he should be king of all Norway in your stead."

And then the messenger fell silent, trembling uncontrollably, but still standing on two feet, his work finished.

King Erik did not appear to be listening anymore however, much less appreciating the Herculean efforts of his messenger. His old falcon was now trying unsuccessfully to pounce upon a little shoot of green that poked up from the snow. The king watched its progress for a short time, and then he said, "Fetch me that bird."

The king's four servants, Bikki One, Bikki Two, Bikki Three, and Bikki Four, ran out into the field. These were the four servants closest to king—his henchmen—known collectively, of course, as the Bikki. They rode closest to him in battle and they were the ones who attended him whenever he went out hunting. They tended to do everything together, no single one of them ever acting independently. This gave them a show of strength all together, but it had been so long since an individual among them had stood alone, either on the battlefield or in his own mind, that it was likely that the four of them together did not even possess the strength of a single small child standing alone with one independent thought to serve as a guide. Take, for example, the task before them now. They run out into the field, onto the crest of the low hill, and approach the bird, cautiously, fearfully, all four of them, while the bird is so intent on his efforts to pounce on a sprig of greenery that he doesn't even notice them. Nor do they notice that he does not notice them, so it takes them almost forever, an eternity of sneakiness, to step gingerly up behind him and slip the black bejewelled hood over his head. His eyes enveloped now by darkness, he immediately ceases all activity and sits rigid and still. You would think that this would be enough to set the Bikki at ease, but it is not so. Together now they coax the falcon up onto a great leather gauntlet, eyes wide with collective terror over the closeness of the claws. They get him up onto a wrist — someone's, it hardly matters whose, they must have flipped a coin over it — and then they breathe a collective sigh of relief, since, despite this bird's obvious feebleness, it is the very singularity of the being that terrifies them most. The task complete, they return to the place at the edge of the field where the king stands.

"A skier," said the king to all those assembled. "I am expected to fear a skier. My name is Erik Blood-Axe and the Tronds of Trondheim expect me to be afraid of a man with sliding feet. How shall I respond to these Tronds of Trondheim and their new, just king?"

He mused for a moment.

"This is what I think: a man who walks with sliding feet, like a falcon without his feathers, is weak."

Then he spoke directly to the falcon. This was something he did not normally do. In fact, the bird had been given a name by King Erik's father, but Erik had long since forgotten what its name was, if he ever knew in the first place. Such minor matters as the proper names of creatures held no interest for him.

"You have served me longest, falcon, and my father before me — fifteen years or more. No longer do you have the eyes of a falcon, or the claws of a falcon, or the beak of a falcon, or the coat of a falcon. And that, as far as I can tell, makes you not a falcon, or hardly one at all."

And then the king did a terrible thing. With a great cry that made the Bikki tremble, the messenger quake, and even the groom stir a little, Erik seized the hooded bird and tore the feathers from his wings and his back. So old were these feathers, like a tattered, old woolen blanket, so matted had they become, gathering dust and old spider's webbing from long hours hooded on a castle perch, so like a coat that had grown over the whole of his life to keep him warm in this cold climate, that like a coat they came off the back of the bird, all in one piece, terrible to behold. A cloak that had warmed him, protected him, and granted him dignity and stature, served as his shield, and inspired him in wild whirls of flight, high in the sky in the days long ago when the sun had shone brilliantly and everywhere. Off came this cloak, and now he was nearly featherless and naked, nearly like a human, under the cloudy sky, the bones of his former wings exposed and hanging at his sides, not like wings at all anymore, but like skinny, double-jointed arms. I don't want to describe it anymore. It was the most awful thing I ever witnessed, though I must confess I do recall another aspect to what I saw. It is possible that I remember now how this indignity may have granted the bird a kind of grandeur that he had not yet possessed—beyond age, beyond experience. Could I be imagining it?

Perhaps I speak too soon of that. For now the bird seemed no more than a collection of bones and a beak; it seemed miraculous to say he was even alive, but he was. The king tossed the bird back onto the servant's gauntlet and spoke to the messenger in a terrible voice.

"Take this old and useless bird to my brother, Haakon the Good. This servant will attend you."

And here he singled out one, single, only, much startled Bikki.

"Tell my brother he is as fit to be a king as this unfeathered bird is fit to be a bird of prey. Tell him I will meet him in battle on the Fields of Snorre tomorrow night. If he does not meet me there, I will sack him before the next morning in his home, and raise such fires as will melt all the snow in his so-called skiing grounds."

And then he shouted the very clear and long remembered words of war:

Hands shall grip the handshafts
Brandish the icicles of blood!
King are you, Haakon my brother?
Well Northern king you'll only be,
If you wake the ways of war with me!

Then he turned and strode away, making great
holes in the snow with his feet as he walked. Three of
his servants stumbled behind him. The fourth, who
had been singled out because he held the bird—the
loser of a coin toss—and held the bird still, stood for a
moment and watched them go. Then he turned and
looked at the messenger, whose eyes were open wide.
After a few moments, the field was clear of all but these
two men and their horses. They looked for all the
world as plucked and helpless as the half-dead bird
they held between them. They wanted nothing more
than to drop this creature and run for the hills of
Denmark. But they had been given orders by their
king, and they feared him more than anything else in
the world. So after a few moments in which the two
contemplated their sorry fate, they groaned a groan
together, sighed a few sighs, turned and plodded over
to their horses.

See the scene before you now: I remember it as if it were
yesterday, across all these centuries. Two horsemen

44

head through a misty grey day toward the North. An
old falcon, hardly recognizable as such, sits perched on
the back of a saddle. He turns his head in small movements. The beak of a falcon is not formed to speak any
human language. All he can utter is "Ak." But if he could
speak to you, faraway reader, in this moment, if he knew
you were there with him on the bone-chilling trail to
the forest, these are the words that he would say:

Hearken you who speak the English tongue,
How a loyal bird is treated when he is old.
Oh yes, it's true: when up in the sky I can forget
That things on the ground are larger than they appear.
I take an outhouse for a mouse and bust up my beak!
But once — oh, once!
When feathers were black and sleek and days were
    bright and green,
I was not some old bird then, but the finest falcon!
    A Peregrine!

5

The Ten-Foot Oaf

THE ONLY PROBLEM was Freya didn't know how to get her hands on a pigeon. The hut was simple enough, for she had been able to build it in a single afternoon from the remains of the old man's. The net was simple enough, since in this country of endless winter her father's few sheep produced more wool than anyone knew what to do with. The village of Trondheim to the north already had stockpiles of wool sweaters in case somebody needed a new one. Their prices were so low that nobody bothered to sell them anymore, yet still her father's sheep produced more wool. They produced so much wool that from a single sheep standing by her loom Freya was able to weave a net as strong as any self-respecting falcon-catcher could wish for. That took three more afternoons. The rope was even easier to produce. One afternoon. The pigeon remained a problem, though. A pigeon was not something one could weave from a sheep's back. Did not all pigeons live in England? Were they not shipped on longboats to Norway at enormous cost? This is what Freya thought. Whether it was true or not, it was certainly true for her, since there was not a pigeon to be had in the whole of her forest. Freya had to find some other way.

One afternoon, just about a week after she had discovered her vocation, Freya was standing in her clearing deep in thought. She had set up the net as best she could, tied one thin length of rope to it, and stood contemplating the other in the centre of the clearing. What, she wondered, could she tie, in lieu of a pigeon, to the end of this rope?

Just then — just as Freya was thinking that she might have begun to form the beginning of a glimmer of a hope of an idea in her mind — Rolf, her great, giant, ten-foot oaf of a brother, came striding by, heading nowhere in particular as usual.

"Rolf!" she cried, "You've interrupted my thoughts!"

"Huh?" asked Rolf, looking around as he strode to see where the voice was coming from. Rolf was such a clumsy nine-year-old that to stop looking where he was going for even a moment was a very grave matter, and this time was no different. As soon as he left off looking, his great leg got caught up in the rope, and tangled, and then he fell, and as he fell, his foot tugged the rope, and since the end of the rope was in Freya's hand, Freya was given a tug, too. She keeled over and landed flat on her face.

"Oh!" cried Rolf, who rarely spoke more than one word at a time. His memory was too full of too many things: so many moments shared with his sister and his father—and other things too; secret things that they knew nothing about, going all the way back to when he was born and sometimes, he thought, before. He often felt and thought and knew so many things at once that it was impossible to express them. And so he preferred to keep silent. Or to speak as little as possible. And so, while you (like Freya) might think he was merely foolish and slow for saying only "oh" when she fell flat on her face, rest assured there was more going on than that.

Still, the fact that you know the truth does nothing to change his behaviour in the moment.

"Oh!" cried Rolf again, who saw what he had done and was trying to get away. But his great tree-trunk legs were now hopelessly tangled and he realized that he was helpless before his sister's wrath. Freya lay very still, flat on her face for a long moment, and then suddenly sprang to her feet. "Oh!" cried Rolf again, but, to his great surprise, he saw that there was no wrath in his sister's eyes. On her face there was not the angry scowl that Rolf had long come to expect, but rather the expression of a kind of—almost—could it be? Gratitude? Perhaps to say it was gratitude is going too far, but certainly one could perceive the warm glow of young genius at its most exultant.

"Rolf!" she cried. "Rolf! I sing of Rolf the Strong and Big! Rolf the Rope-Puller! Rolf the Great! Rolf the Counterweight!"

Rolf had never heard his sister speak in this way before. Her words sounded full of praise, and they brought tears of joy immediately to his eyes. For if truth be told, it saddened and mortified Rolf that he made his sister so angry so much of the time. He had long wished for nothing more purely and simply than to be made small again, so that he and she could once again sit quietly behind the bushes of the forest and watch the creatures go about their daily business. He had long understood that this would never happen, and was unhappy to have grown into a great clumsy oaf. To be suddenly praised for his size was a miracle beyond reckoning, and he was even less prepared for what came next.

"Get up, Rolf!" cried Freya. "Untangle yourself. I want you to help me."

Well now. Rolf was so surprised by his sister's command that he forgot all about his various entanglements and stood up. As he did so, calmly and with colossal dignity, the rope that had been twisted around his legs fell easily and harmlessly to the ground, and he stepped out of it.

"Come here, Rolf," said Freya, with glorious authority, "and follow my instructions carefully, for I am Freya the Falcon-Catcher, and we have much to accomplish this afternoon."

Rolf's eyes widened. His sister had just said "we." Imagine that: "we." To hear his sister say "we" was beyond everything he had wished for. Beyond anything he had hoped for. Despite the grey landscape, the world for him was suddenly bright and new and full of the possibility of we.

Freya continued: "Normally, Rolf, such work as mine is conducted alone. However, I have been thwarted in my endeavour by the lack of a pigeon. Imagine being lost for the lack of a single pigeon. I am one pigeon poor, and one is enough. But for a single pigeon, I would even now be walking through the halls of Erik, Great King of Norway."

Rolf had never heard his sister speak with such high style or seriousness. She shone with a new mystery in the afternoon light. Certainly, he had never heard her speak of kings and pigeons. He listened with rapt attention.

"You are big, Rolf, and I am not. Therefore, necessity demands that, until I acquire a true pigeon to serve as bait, I must myself take its place in the trap I have built. For though I am Freya the Bold, I am also Freya the Small. Small enough, to be sure, for me to play the part of a pigeon. You, on the other hand, though you can be Rolf the Oaf, are also Rolf the Big. You must therefore become my apprentice, and stand in my place as falcon-catcher. I shall sit here in this clearing and you will sit crouched inside that hut. Stretched between us will be a long piece of twine. One end will be tied around my waist and the other end will be held in your hand. In your other hand will be another length of twine. When a great sun-touched falcon swoops down to take the bait, I will give you a signal. On my signal you will pull hard on both lengths of twine. The first will yank me out of harm's way, and the second will cause the falcon to be engulfed in a net. Do you understand what I'm saying to you?"

Rolf nodded.

"And then, Rolf, together you and I will take our bird to the king. You and I will bend our knees, and I will raise our bird on my gloved wrist, and so we will all become honoured servants of the king."

Rolf's great lantern jaw was hanging open on its hinges, and his knees buckled a little with excitement as Freya continued to instruct him and he continued to nod his head in agreement. With his sister leading the way, he was ready to try anything. So many new thoughts whirled around his head that he was almost delirious with anticipation for their adventures: Rolf the Big. Freya the Small. Freya the pigeon. Rolf the Apprentice. Freya the Falcon-Catcher. Freya and Rolf, brother and sister forever. Freya and Rolf, honoured servants of the king.

6

The World Beyond

TWO HORSEMEN head through a cloudy grey afternoon, toward a forest just south of Trondheim. They're almost there. Fixed to the saddle of one horse there is a makeshift perch. On the perch, an old hooded falcon, friendless, shorn of feathers, reflects upon his life and rediscovers his strength. There is strength, he finds, in the coiled muscles of his legs and talons, in the keenness of his hearing, in the weight of all he knows from his long life. Sometimes it takes a terrible action to introduce a creature to himself. This bird has been so introduced.

In all the centuries that falcons have had their heads hooded to trick them into believing that it is night, never before this moment, or even since, has there been a bird that learned the truth. Although this bird has a hood designed by the finest craftsman of Persia to fit around his skull like a second skin; although his hood is composed of the most tightly woven silk, produced by the silkworms and weavers of the northernmost regions of China to sell and to keep themselves warm; although it was once dipped by Mediterranean dyers into a vat of the inkiest black dye, in which all daylight was subsumed and not a ray could escape; although this falcon is hooded with such a hood, still he knows it is day.

A Capture

ROLF WAS NO LONGER NODDING. He was shaking his head. Vigorously. His shaggy locks were swaying from side to side, slapping him in the forehead. Everything was happening at once. It was one thing to have the workings of the falcon trap explained to Rolf, but it was quite another for him to see it set up and be himself a part of it. He was leaning against the hut—which had originally been built by Freya for herself to sit inside and so was, of course, much too small for him—and holding the end of the rope. His sister was thirty feet or so away from him, tied to the other end. And once again, as if nothing had ever changed, Freya was yelling at him.

"No! Rolf! Little brother! Pull it taut! Taut!"

The rope stayed slack in his hand. He did not want

to hurt her by pulling too hard.

"You must pull the rope taut, Rolf! Like this!"

She yanked on the rope and it came roughly out of Rolf's gentle hands. Freya was so frustrated that she was almost turning blue.

"Pick that up!"

Rolf picked it up. Freya tried to speak more calmly.

"Rolf, you have to learn how to use the strength in your hands and your arms. You're big—look how big you are! You can do it. I know you can do it."

Rolf shook his head. Rolf didn't want to be big. Not now or ever. Freya kept talking.

"You're not going to hurt me, you know. Do you think you're going to hurt me?"

Rolf nodded. Freya sighed.

"I already explained to you about the pigeon, Rolf. If we had a pigeon, then I could do your job and you wouldn't even have to be here. But you want to be here, don't you?"

Rolf nodded.

"Good. Good, Rolf! I thought so. So, all you have to do is brace yourself and keep the rope taut."

Rolf braced himself and gave the rope a little tug, just strong enough to pull Freya one step forward.

"Good, Rolf! Excellent! That was excellent! See how that didn't hurt me one little bit?"

Rolf nodded, relieved to be nodding again.

"Try it again."

Rolf gave the rope another meek little tug, and

again Freya was pulled a step forward. Once again she expressed her satisfaction to Rolf, but Rolf was no longer listening. His attention had been lured away by the sight of something moving through the distant woods behind his older sister. It seemed to be moving at great speed, as if it were flying, but it was very low to the ground and—of even greater interest—it seemed to be coming straight for them. It looked very strange and bony for a bird, but a bird was the only thing it really could be—a bird with skewed white tree branches poking from its sides instead of wings. Rolf cocked his head to try and get a better look. In an instant of temper, Freya saw that her little brother was no longer listening to her. Her eyes widened and she was just about to launch into a pack of insults, such as had never been heard in the whole history of the North, but—and this was difficult for her to admit to herself—there was something about his expression that made her curious. He was so puzzled, it was clear even from thirty feet away. What could make Rolf so curious as to stop paying attention and risk the censure of his older sister? She couldn't help herself and turned to look.

And then she screamed.

There was an enormous falcon, skittering low through the wintry wood. His wings, such as they were, were spread wide and he appeared to be trying to take off, but something was preventing him. There was an air of desperation about the way he ran, his talons clipped the ground like small spades and he seemed always about to crash into the next tree trunk. In a moment, he was through the trees and into the clearing, heading straight through the centre, and the only obstacle in his path was Freya herself — Freya the pigeon.

Freya wheeled to face Rolf, suddenly feeling very much as helpless as a pigeon. Rolf, who had never seen a falcon close up before, was frozen to the spot.

"Rolf! Pull the rope! Rolf! Pull the rope! Pull the rope, Rolf! Rolf! PULL THE ROPE NOW!"

Freya turned from the frozen Rolf just as the falcon careened blindly into her. Rolf yelped as the bird and the girl went tumbling forward together in the snow. Looking at the ropes in his two hands, he realized in an instant that he had left his duty woefully undone, and, as afraid of not doing as of doing, he closed his eyes and pulled. A net dropped down from the trees and engulfed the tumbling pair. "Oh!" cried Rolf. "Oh! Oh! Oh!"

Freya and the bird were tangled together in the net. As the enormous bird silently struggled, Freya managed to pull herself away from it. She pulled the edge of the net out from over her and crawled away, out into the snow. Then she jumped to her feet, ran over to Rolf, and began slapping him about the shins.

"You addlehead!" she cried. "You madcap! You moron! Why didn't you pull the rope?"

Rolf was frightened of the bird and frightened of

Freya and relieved that Freya was safe and recoiling from the smarting smacks that were being delivered to his poor shins, all in the same moment. He was also feeling ashamed of himself. "I was scared," he said, in a small, reedy voice.

Freya was momentarily taken aback by her brother's use of three different words in a row, but then she launched straight back into her shin-smacking rampage.

"You were scared? How do you think I felt falling into a net with that great big bloodthirsty bird? How do you think I felt, tangled up with that tough old wild-caught haggard? Huh?"

Rolf shrugged his great shoulders as meekly as he could. As usual, he didn't have the slightest idea what he could say or do to appease his enraged sister, but, in fact, Freya was already beginning to calm down. The fact of her success was occurring to her. It was dawning on her that she had caught herself a falcon, that there was a falcon in the net, that he had stopped struggling, that he was sitting very still, over there in the centre of the clearing, underneath her net. She had caught a falcon. The falcon was hers. The first step of her grand plan had been completed. She was Freya the Falcon-Catcher. Now all that was left to do was ... now there was merely the simple matter of ... well, ah, of ...

Of what? How was Freya going to train this falcon, a wild falcon, to become a hunting falcon, a noble falcon that stood perched upon her wrist? How was she going to train this falcon to understand that it was his job to sit very still upon her wrist, while she marched into the main hall of Norway and presented her captive to the king? How does one go about doing such things? She had modelled all her actions up to this point on the behaviour of the old man with the long nose, but the last thing she saw him do was poke his bird-sack with his nose and tell the falcon that he was going to train him to be a servant of the king. But she never actually saw him train the falcon to be the servant of the king. How on earth does a person train a falcon to go and be a servant of the king? She didn't have the slightest idea. It seemed suddenly like the most impossible notion: birds were birds, and people were people. How does the one train the other to do anything at all?

And there were other problems, too: this falcon was actually bigger than she was. It looked like there weren't going to be any falcons perched on any gloved wrist of hers, not unless she grew overnight to be as big as Rolf. And what if this was a bad falcon? What if this falcon was already well-known for being a wild thief of hens and chickens and geese? What if she returned home in triumph with this falcon, only to have her father, in a fit of clear-sightedness, recognize it as the most infamous chicken-thief in the region, take it right out of her hands and send it away to be tried for its crimes before the hallowed magistrates of Trondheim?

She didn't know what to do. Or rather, there was

only one thing to do: there was one more action of the old needle-nosed man that she could emulate before the darkness descended over her knowledge of falconry. Making her decision, she turned away from the red-smacked shins of Rolf and marched back into the centre of the clearing, where the falcon was still sitting very still underneath his net. She marched right up to the net and crouched so that her nose was very close to the bird. Her mind blanked for a moment and she didn't know what to say, but then she thought again of the old falcon-catcher in the woods, and so she spoke, boldly and directly, the only authoritative words she could think of speaking:

"Have you killed hens, you devil?"

Morton

HIS NAME WAS MORTON, this falcon, and the loss of a good portion of the feathers on his wings and back, not to mention the skin that held them together, had left him feeling more than a little irritated. "Where is the justice in that?" he had thought to himself as he crouched into a spring from his position on the makeshift perch on the back of the servant's saddle. "What thanks have I been given today for all my years of loyal service?" he had asked himself as he hopped lightly off the saddle and onto the head of the horse's human rider. "Perhaps I should have been allowed to retire," he had affirmed to himself as he tore out patches of the screaming servant's hair. "I should have been given a tall tree—" as he knocked the servant out of his saddle and jumped over to the messenger's horse, "that stood so tall I could have perched on a branch higher than the clouds — " as he made short work of the second rider, "and spent my last remaining days basking in the sun," as he jumped down and clutched at the snow with his talons.

Then he was earthbound and running blind. Though he could not see the devastation of his body, still he knew he couldn't fly. So he spread his featherless wings for balance and skittered and glided and ran as fast as he could, the sharp tips of his talons finding purchase in the spongy earth. A desperate and wilful creature will find new ways of doing things, and Morton had found a unique and effective way for a blind and flightless bird to travel. What a spectacular wreckage he was! A great old white bird with pure white plumes across his stomach, flecked with black, stripped gooseflesh across his back and a spread wingspan of exposed bones, head sewn up in a hood, barrelling over the countryside like a badly made flying machine. Any birdwatcher that might have been out that afternoon would have been given a sight such as he had never seen before, and such as he would never see again if he lived and watched birds for the rest of his days.

Morton did not know in what direction he ran, except that for a short while the riderless horses ran with him. He heard the angry cries of the men behind him falling back into the distance, and he felt with some sixth sense that he was heading toward a large wooded area. This sense of approaching shelter had barely manifested itself upon his heart when, a moment later, he felt great shadows all around him. He was within the trees. He heard their sigh. He heard the wind whistle through their needles. He sensed their enormous trunks everywhere around and in front of him. He knew that perhaps he should slow down, blind as he was, but he was a stubborn old falcon, and his stubborn old will kept him skittering at top speed. That same sixth sense that had told him of the trees seemed also to keep him from crashing into them. Faulty apparatus will serve a skilled pilot nonetheless, and Morton was a skilled old pilot. No longer was he the bored and listless bird he'd been — the bird that had lacked the will to do his master's bidding and bag a pheasant or two. After all, he thought to himself, why should he have done that? Why should he have bothered to bag a fowl for King Erik? He was glad he had defied the king, even though it had made him look like an incompetent hunter, even though it had lost him his wings, even though it had nearly killed him. To have bagged a bird would have only whetted the king's appetite, and the whole nauseating task would have had to be carried out all over again, the next day and the day after that and the day after that. The gluttonous tyrant never even shared his catch with anyone — he certainly didn't share it with Morton. No more, Morton resolved as he ran, would this old falcon ever do the bidding of any king. Kingship was a bad business.

It seemed mostly like a children's game to him, not at all a serious pursuit for adults. It was a sport for cruel boys. As for the role of the falcons, why, they were meant for soaring above the clouds, and he resolved in his heart to soar again before his days were through.

Still, as he ran, he tried to control the panic that was rising with so many questions inside him: How would he ever get that hood off? Would he live forever in darkness? Would he ever be able to fly again? Were there any friends to be had in such a world as this, where kings tore the wings off of their loyal servants? He told himself that he would find a fellow falcon, or an osprey or a goshawk, and that this fellow bird would peck at the bindings at the back of his head until the hood fell away and restored his sight. He ran without a thought as to where he was running, with only the thought that he was running away, and that ahead of him lay a life that he couldn't begin to imagine even if he had the time.

Then he hit something. It came as a complete surprise because it had seemed to him that he was running through a clearing and was, for the moment, free of the danger of trees. Just after he entered the clearing however he had heard the cry of an animal coming from some-where in front of him, and suddenly his pilot's apparatus seemed to fail: too late he tried to change direction and then he stumbled into a form, which, though quite a bit smaller than any tree, knocked him off his balance and sent him tumbling.

A small package of paws and cries poked and flailed at him as they rolled in a tight bundle through the snow. He pulled his bony wings over himself for protection, but they covered the creature too, and it yelped and clutched at him, scratching and screeching as together they continued to tumble endlessly. The general, overall sensation was one of great unpleasantness, and he wished that he could come to a stop. No sooner had he made this wish than it was granted in a manner decidedly not to his taste, for it was accompanied by a sensation that he had long remembered from his earliest days—one of his earliest memories, in fact—that of being enclosed within a net. The feeling of the mesh would have inspired panic within him were he not already so overwhelmed with irritation. The thought that he had escaped the clutches of the most powerful man in the land only to run straight into some falcon-catcher's net set his beak on edge. This falcon-catcher, he thought, was going to regret he had ever wandered into these woods. And if being caught wasn't bad enough, Morton had been caught with a mewling, poking, clawing little monster that was, even now, scrabbling over his chest. The thing was poking and pushing at his head with an almost childlike ferocity, and Morton was just about to start pecking back when it suddenly crawled off of him and was gone.

Now that Morton was alone in the net, he realized that he liked this even less. At least with the creature for company he could have bargained with it—once it had calmed down. Together they might have discovered some clever means of thwarting the intentions of their captor. Left alone, however, he found that his bindings only screwed in more securely when he struggled. He stopped and lay very still, trying to catch his breath. One spindly wing was spread awkwardly over his stomach, where it had earlier been caught against the creature, and he attempted to manoeuvre it around and fold it neatly over his back where it belonged. Once this was accomplished, he lay still and composed himself for what was to come.

9

Meeting of Minds

"HAVE YOU KILLED HENS, you devil?"

Morton had never been called a devil before, though he knew that in his unfeathered, disheveled state he must surely resemble one. Still, he felt compelled to give the small-sounding creature that addressed him the benefit of the doubt. "I beg your pardon?" he asked.

There was a pause. A pause caused by the fact that Freya, though she had spoken to her captive bird and asked him a direct question, had not actually expected to be answered. Never in her whole life had she imagined that a bird could speak. She stuttered out her reply:

"I . . . I said . . . I asked you if you have killed hens . . . well . . . because my father keeps hens, and he says a bird is a bad bird if that bird has killed hens. If you have killed hens then I must reject you as a hunting falcon and kill you outright."

Now it was Morton's turn to be surprised, for it had become apparent to him—by her words and the way she spoke them—that the tiny creature who addressed him was a human: a human who was, in fact, a young female; a human who had a parent who kept hens, and that this same young female human was the very same human who had captured him in this very same infernal net. The thing that was most strange about this human little girl was that she seemed well versed in the language of falcons, a skill he had never imagined any normal human to be even remotely capable of. Still, he was, for the moment, overwhelmed with indignation at her accusation of murder and thievery, and so he let pass this matter of the girl's conversational grasp of his native tongue.

"No, I have not killed hens, you impertinent child," said Morton. "Where, I ask you, is the skill in that? Where's the chase in bagging a domestic farm animal, penned in and fat? Anyway, in case you haven't noticed, I could not kill anything in the state I'm in— not even you."

"Well, I doubt that, you trickster," said Freya, who had so far failed to notice the peculiar handicaps of this bird. "I doubt that very much."

The hooded Morton was still very puzzled. Here in front of him was a clearly idiotic, unobservant little girl who spoke masterful falcon. There were many thousands of bird languages—he himself spoke seven, including grouse, pheasant, goshawk, and sparrow. He had, in fact, had several civil conversations with the sparrows that lived under the eaves of the longhouse that had been his home all these years. Suppressing a sudden throb at the thought that he would never return to that place, he wondered if this human female spoke only the one bird language, or whether she knew many. Perhaps she knew them all!

"Who are you?" he asked, finally. "You sound like some young girl. Of whom were you born, girl, that you could snare the agewisest falcon in the land?"

Freya tried to muster up some mettle before her savage captive. "I am Freya the Falcon-Catcher, peasant-born."

"Oh, a falcon-catcher are you?" said Morton. "Well, that explains everything. I must ask then that you remove this hood, so that I might view my oh-so-noble captor with these, my own eyes."

Freya was taken aback. She looked over at Rolf, who had crept forward. His mouth was open and he had a queer expression on his face, but he wasn't peering at the falcon as she expected, but rather at her. "What are you looking at?" she thought to herself, and then turned back to the matter at hand. Peering beneath the fabric of the net before her, she saw finally that her captive was indeed hooded and blind.

"How can you be hooded?" she asked, somewhat peevishly despite her undeniable curiosity. "How came you to be hooded and flying through this wood?"

"Oh, mysterious is it?" countered the old bird. "Well, it doesn't seem to me to be the most mysterious thing that is happening this afternoon. In any case, if you'd bothered to look at me when I ran into you, you would have seen that I was not flying at all. I don't know how you might describe what it was that I was doing, but it was most certainly not flying."

"The greatest mystery is the fact that you were moving at all!" said Freya. "For I know that instinct should forbid a hooded bird from stepping off his perch."

"Unless that hooded bird is a desperate bird, and has escaped the clutches of the king."

"King Erik?"

"The same. Show me my perch in a time of peace and I will step onto it and not stir," said the falcon.

Freya stood up straight from her crouch. Everything suddenly made sense to her. A hooded bird that was capable, she thought, of human speech: What else could he be but a servant of the Great King of Norway? A king so great that he had the knowledge and the authority to bring master teachers from the ends of the earth, who were skilled in teaching birds to speak Norse and the other human tongues? Excitement swelled inside her, such as she had not felt since she had witnessed the old catcher in the forest. She spoke again to the bird with all the authority she could muster: "You have escaped from King Erik, have you? Then he will be pleased to get you back!"

Freya turned to her brother, who had crept still closer, and practically sang with delight: "Rolf! We're going to the longhouse of the king! Of Freya's most bold bagging of this hawk, his poets will surely sing!"

If falcons could turn pale, Morton most surely would have in this moment of his captor's joyful declaration. At the mention of King Erik, he felt a cloud pass over his heart that pulled him deeper into his age.

"No," he said with simple dignity. "If there is anything that is good inside you, you will not return me to the king. He will punish me."

"Of course he will punish you, since you have escaped!" pronounced Freya, who tried as hard as she could, these days at least, to always be of practical mind and to pay as little attention as possible to her heart. "That is only natural. That is the way of things. Anyway, it is little concern of mine what he may choose to do. He is the king. If I am to be a great falcon-catcher, my first duty must always be to the king!"

Morton shivered and spoke flatly, "Oh hail, great falcon-catcher, who would be servant to the foulest king that ever lived. Oh hail, great falcon-catcher, who would rather prostrate herself before an evil, selfish, cruel man than live in the woods wherein she was born, daughter to a humble peasant and the equal of all living creatures."

"I don't understand what you're talking about," said Freya. "Of course I have no wish to stay in these woods. Who would? Mind your own business, falcon. Of course I have no wish to be merely the daughter of a peasant. Especially a peasant as mad as my father."

"Well I'd be a madman too, if I had a daughter as cruel as you," said Morton bitterly. And before Freya could respond to this stinging accusation, he continued. "And you are a foolish young female and as mad as your father if you would put yourself purposely in the path of such a king. What if I told you that this king joys in the fact that our land, which was once so pleasant and green, is now covered with a misery of snow, and that our sky, which was once blue and blazing with the proud sun, is now cloaked over with clouds?"

"I—" Freya was taken aback by this. How could this falcon have so easily guessed her deepest feelings in the matter of her surroundings? Her feelings about the perpetual winter in Norway must have been more common than she had ever thought if they were shared by a creature so different from herself as this falcon from the royal household. Then again, a falcon—composed as he is of sunlight and shadow—must be the greatest authority on the workings of the sky and the mysteries of its weather. That's why he would share her feelings. Except this was a captive falcon and therefore a wily falcon, and therefore a falcon who would say anything in order to set himself free. Such were the thoughts that whirled around Freya's head as she peered again through the mesh of the net at the falcon's hooded head. She suddenly found herself wondering what might be the colour of his eyes.

"I should not believe you," she said, though she thought she had said, "I do not believe you," as that is what she had meant to say.

"Still, it is so," said the falcon. "Young mistress, please, all you have to do is look at me to see evidence of this king's infernal cruelty. He has torn out my feathers and sent me as an insult, a banner of weakness and a declaration of war, to his usurping brother. This ignoble fate I have only just now escaped, conquering even my fear of darkness and blindness and night. And now I have run into your trap, and now you will return me to this same king. Round and round I go, snared by fate, tied to the Tree of the World and whirling around it, caught in some wild, infernal wind that will never stop until the tree topples and all things come to an end."

Freya was chilled by the bird's depiction of his own fate. A land with a toppled tree at the end of the world sounded like a loveless place. It reminded her of her father's bitter boasts, and to think of her father made her feel sad. For the first time since she had captured the falcon, Freya looked close and saw that his coat was torn and barely covered the flesh of his back. For the first time, she saw the near exposed bones of his wings. What kind of king's servant was this, she thought to herself, that he should have been so abused? Still, he was her prisoner, and the only means she had to improve her lot in life. She thought perhaps it was best not to heed his words any longer, but when he continued she found she could not help but listen.

"Girl," said the falcon, "if you would only consider keeping me for yourself, then I would be a falcon with a falconer and you would be a falconer with a falcon. I would be your loyal servant and your friend, and I would teach you all that I know of the ways of war, and the ways of winged creatures."

"You're lying," said Freya, trying to forget her feelings of empathy. "Birds of prey are vicious killers. They are never loyal. The most any human can hope from them is the respect that is due from the servant to the master."

"Yes, and hooded falcons cannot move. Look at me, young girl. Remove my hood and you will see that I am old. I have nothing left to me but my loyalty. The fight has all but run from these unfeathered bones, but not the skill. As for you, how could I not be loyal to a human like you? You are clearly a special kind of child."

Again Freya found herself wondering what might be the colour of this bird's eyes. Still, she did not trust him, and how much more powerful might he be if she removed his hood. He might then be capable of wending his way out of the net, and then who could tell what he might do? In the meantime, he seemed to have resorted to flattery, and Freya the Bold was not about to be fooled by anything like that. She could flatter herself well enough, thank you very much.

"Why do you call me a special kind of child?" she asked, suspicious, unaware that everything was just about to change for her. "I'm a peasant, perhaps a talented catcher of falcons, but still only the daughter of a goatherd."

"Then tell me, goatherd's daughter," said Morton, "how it came to be that you learned the language of birds."

Freya was taken aback. "What do you mean?"

"Well, listen to yourself: You're speaking to me in my own tongue."

"I am not."

"You are."

Freya scoffed. "I'm not speaking in your language, you're speaking in mine!"

"I have a beak. Your strange human sound cannot pass through it."

"You're just trying to confuse me," said Freya, who was struggling to quell the thrill of possibility in this. Could she really have possession of such a special hidden talent, one of which she wasn't even aware? It was ridiculous, it was a ridiculous claim, it was absolutely ridiculous, it was ridiculous. She turned to her brother.

"Rolf!" she cried. "This bird claims that I have been speaking to him in his own tongue. Tell him he's a liar!"

Rolf continued to stare blankly at his sister, just as he had been doing since she had first approached her quarry. She seemed to him to have gone utterly mad. For the last several minutes, she'd been chattering and whistling in the general direction of the bird, and the bird had been chattering and whistling back, both of them primarily using a word that sounded for all the world like "Ak." "Ak ak ak ak," Freya had said to the bird. "Ak ak ak ak," the bird had said back. "Ak," said Freya. "Ak ak" responded the bird. "Ak ak ak ak ak ak, ak ak akak ak ak ak ak ak," said Freya. Back and forth it went. And now, to top it all off, Freya had turned and was chattering straight at Rolf. By her manner it was clear that she expected him to answer, but he had no idea what answer might be appropriate under the circumstances.

"Ak," he ventured, halfheartedly.

"He doesn't understand you," said Morton to the confused and annoyed Freya. "You've forgotten to switch back to your own tongue."

"Well!" huffed Freya, "How am I supposed to tell the difference between the language of birds and my own human language if they both sound exactly, precisely the same to me?"

"I don't know," said Morton. "Perhaps if you calm down and take a deep breath it might clear a few things up for you. I find that can be very helpful when I want to speak to the sparrows under the eaves of the long-house that has been my lodging."

"Hmmph," replied Freya.

She took a deep breath and looked hard at her brother. "Rolf," she said, and her success was immediately apparent. Rolf smiled and nodded. It was quite a relief to him to learn that his sister had not gone entirely crazy. Then he would have been alone in the whole world.

"Do you understand what I'm saying to you, Rolf?" asked Freya in clearly articulated syllables.

Rolf nodded gladly.

"Did you understand me before when I was speaking to the falcon?"

Rolf paused for a moment and furrowed his brow. Then he shook his head.

"Did you understand the falcon?"

Again Rolf shook his head.

"Hmmm," said Freya, and again she sought to quell the excitement that was building inside her. "This is really the strangest thing that has ever happened to me. Rolf, what did it sound like when I was speaking to the falcon? What did my words sound like?"

Rolf did not need to consider this. "Ak," he said definitively.

"Well," said Freya, turning back to the falcon. "Now I'm very confused. I suppose now it's you who doesn't know what I'm saying."

"Quite the contrary," said Morton. "I understand you very well. It would seem you can make the transition from your language to mine rather effortlessly. It's going in the other direction that needs a bit of work."

"I'll have to work on that," said Freya, quickly glancing at the again bewildered Rolf. She always tried to take new information in her stride. Still, she couldn't help wondering whether there wasn't some kind of magical or devilish trickery going on. Perhaps she was under a spell.

"But why would I know your language?" she asked. "It doesn't make sense. A person can't suddenly know a language just like that, can they?"

"I don't know," said Morton. "Perhaps you've drunk some dragon's blood and did not know it. Dragon's blood has long been considered to have that capacity."

"I think if I had drunk some dragon's blood, I'd have remembered it," said Freya, and stamped her foot in the snow.

"I suppose so, I suppose so," said Morton. "But the fact is, you know my language, and you speak it very well, I might add. You have been somehow blessed. Perhaps...." He paused and then shook his head. "No. That is even more unlikely than the thought of dragon's blood."

"What? What is it?" asked Freya.

"I was going to say that perhaps you are of the tribe they call the Valkyries of which the ancient Edda tells."

"What is a 'Valkyrie'?" asked Freya, who didn't know what an "Edda" was either, though that seemed not so important as this thing called a Valkyrie.

"I will, in good time, tell you everything you wish to know about Valkyries," said Morton, "and more besides. If you are indeed from that tribe, it would explain much about your talents. It would also mean that there is much you would be able to learn from me."

"I don't know how I can come to trust a falcon that I've caught in a net," said the suspicious Freya. "It seems to me he would say anything to get himself free."

"Then there is nothing I can say to dispel your mistrust," said Morton, who realized that he was indeed going to have to do a little scheming if he was going to get himself set free. "I have said all I can."

"Tell me one thing I can learn from you."

"But have I not already taught you a thing or two?" asked the falcon.

"Such things could be lies or witches' spells," said Freya. "Tell me one real thing I could learn from you — something practical."

"Well, my cautious one," said Morton, who would have furrowed his brow if he had a brow to furrow, "I could teach you how to divine future events by looking at tracks in the snow."

"But tracks in the snow tell only past events."

"Yes, they do that too, but if you know how to look, events that take place in the wild wood will foretell events in your human realm."

"I don't believe you."

"Remove my hood. I'll show you."

"How do I know you won't try to — ?"

"If you don't trust me then leave me tangled in the net while you remove my hood. I'm sure I can easily show you from here."

Freya had reached the moment of decision. She looked at her captive in the net. What feathers he had were snowy white. Tangled up as he was, he looked as frail as an old goose; not nearly the threat that she imagined a falcon should be. She reached in, somewhat tentatively given the sharpness of his beak, and untangled his hooded head from the net. Then she reached around, untied the leather thongs, and pulled the hood forward off the falcon's gnarled beak.

Morton blinked and looked at her and she saw his eyes. His eyes were a dull gold colour, like the sun covered with the thinnest wisp of cloud. There was clearly intelligence locked within them—world-weariness, wisdom—but Freya was struck by the fact that, though she understood his words, she was unable to read any expression on his face whatsoever. It was a noble face, with a crown of black feathers and proud yellow nostrils, and a beak that began grey against ochre, but was black as a slash of midnight at its tip. It was as unfamiliar to her as the sky above the clouds, and its otherness overwhelmed her understanding. Only time would tell whether she would be able to say whether it was smiling, or frowning, or deep in thought. For now, he simply filled her with awe. Was this the creature she'd been talking to for all this time? She turned to look at Rolf, to see if he was watching. Her brother was sitting down against a tree trunk, snoring softly, looking very much like the young boy he really was, despite his size.

"Hmmph," said the falcon, struck by Freya's brown eyes and the half-moon circles beneath them. "I suppose you've never seen a bird of prey up close before."

Freya shook her head. Morton opened his beak

and laughed, a sudden, sharp kind of *rat-tat-tat* that shocked her. "That's an unfortunate confession for you to be making," he exclaimed, "considering you call yourself Freya the Falcon-Catcher, peasant-born."

"You were to have been my first falcon," said Freya softly, still in awe of the bird's dull golden eyes.

"I was to have been and I am," said Morton. "I am, though I'm afraid I may need a bit of fixing up if I am to be someone's first falcon. Now, look here: I see something already."

The falcon was looking intently over at the snow by the edge of the clearing. Freya followed his eyes.

"Look over there; I see by those tracks that two rabbits were here."

Morton, I hate to say it, was wily after all—wilier than he had let on with all his lulling of his young captor. Now that he had the aid of his eyes, he was easily able to free himself from the net and hop out into the open. Freya, for all her caution, had failed to notice, since in order to see what Morton had claimed to observe with his powerful falcon eyes, she'd had to wander over to the edge of the clearing and was now crouching over the rabbit tracks that turned out really to have been there.

Morton quickly glanced over at the girl's giant brother, who was lying asleep under a tree. He realized that he was free to go. Now that his sight had been returned to him, there was nothing that this girl or this boy or anyone else, for that matter, could do to prevent him from skittering away to freedom. The human female had been right after all: the bird of prey will feel no loyalty, merely the respect due to the master that keeps and feeds it. Once set free, he is wild once more.

Morton swung open his tattered wings, to provide himself with balance. He was already free, in fact. He was as good as gone.

10

A Falcon Finds a Falconer

EVEN AS CHILDREN, we feel there is a part of ourselves, inside ourselves, that seems to us to be very old and very wise. Is that not true? Perhaps I'm so old that I truly have grown, finally, senile, and I don't remember anything properly anymore. It seems to me that this wisdom is like a voice inside us, and sometimes we listen to this voice and sometimes we don't. If we listen to it as we grow—speak with it, hear it hum within the chambers of our hearts—then the voice will grow beyond the hum and come to occupy our outer selves more and more, until, when we are old, it may just become impossible to distinguish between our outer self and our wiser self. This is wishful thinking, I suppose. For Morton, a hunting hawk, such a simple growth toward wisdom would have been hardly possible.

His had been the harsh life of a servant, and such a temperate inner voice would have been of little use. "Spare the little pheasant." He could not. "Spare the little grouse." He would suffer for it. "Let the goshawk have the spoils." Why, that would be foolish, and Morton would go hungry. "Learn the language of the sparrows." Well, there's nothing wrong with that, is there? Perhaps he would. Do you see what I mean? Sometimes he would heed the inner voice; often he would not.

And so when a small quiet voice spoke inside Morton, it was as surprising and unfamiliar as it would be to any child. As he spread his wings to skitter away from the clearing with its ropes and its nets and its guileless young humans—as he felt the full flight of his freedom though he knew he could not take to the air—Morton cast a sidelong glance in the direction of his former captor.

And then the small and unfamiliar voice spoke inside him: "This one speaks the language of birds, after all. Haven't you told her you have so much to teach her? Perhaps not so much, but enough?"

Morton blinked. The girl was now standing at the edge of the clearing and was looking at him. Her mouth was hanging open like one who knew she had just been tricked, and her face bore an open expression of loss. It affected her with a sadness and a dignity that made her seem suddenly older. Her eyes, grown accustomed to watching the backs of those who turned away from her: a sad father with his goats, mocking school-mates returning to their play, the silhouettes of the women in the trees heading always toward the north, Rolf turning tail to flee in fear from his very own sister. And now the falcon who was to have brought her glory.

Morton turned his head and looked as far as he could toward the deepest regions of the wood. Solitary freedom. He was poised to go. He was master of his own fate. He looked at the girl again, and back at the distant wood. And then he spoke.

"Yes, it's just as I thought."

"What?" she responded, sadly. "What is it that you've thought?"

In an instant, he was by her side and peering into the scuffed snow. "Look at this: two rabbits were here. And an owl."

Freya felt a wave of gratitude roll over her.

"The owl seems to have swooped down upon the rabbits," Morton continued, "but, contrary to what you might expect, the owl did not gain the upper hand. There are a few small feathers here in the snow; they look like they've come from the nape of the owl's neck. It's my guess that there was a struggle, and that the rabbits won the day and lived to tell their tale of trouble to instruct their fellows. See there: two sets of foot-prints, running into the forest. Not one, but two. Oh, brave rabbits! Even now, I imagine, their story is being told somewhere in the warrens below us, safely hidden beneath the snow."

Morton's head had been bent low, as close as possible to the tracks and the snow. Now he looked with great satisfaction up into the face of his human companion. Freya felt another wave of gratitude for this bird who had not taken flight in spite of his freedom—not, at any rate, taken to his heels, or his talons, or whatever one might say under the circumstances.

"What is your name?" she asked. "Do you have a name? What is your name?"

"But don't you want to know what it all means?" asked the falcon, returning to his study of the tracks in the snow. "I told you it would foretell events in your human realm."

"All right," said Freya. "Yes. I don't know. Tell me what it means."

"But isn't it obvious?" asked Morton, who looked for all the world like he suddenly had flashed a wry smile. "I think it's really fairly obvious."

"I don't see how anything's obvious at all," said a flustered Freya, hotly. A moment ago she had been thrilled to see that this bird had not fled and thought she might befriend him, but now he was truly displaying the most annoying behaviour. She did not like being toyed with and made to feel stupid. She did not like that at all. Before she could form the words of her anger however, the two of them were suddenly ambushed by a large man with torn patches of hair, who jumped out of the trees.

Ambush

THE KING'S SERVANT'S name was Bikki
Number Four, and, as I have told before, he was
accustomed to conducting all his daily tasks in
the company of the king's other three primary servants —
Bikki Number One, Bikki Number Two and Bikki
Number Three — and wasn't much used to being singled
out for tasks. I can tell you for certain that he'd never
been much fond of falcons or falconry, or even horses
for that matter, so he wasn't really pleased at all when
he got pinned with the task of bearing one wretched
old falcon on the bony back of a wretched horse to the
wretched northern village of Trondheim, which had
made a wretched king out of his master's wretched
brother, to whom he himself had been given the
wretched job of declaring some wretched war.

Nor was he much pleased when that same wretched old falcon, who had been pretty much dead as far as he could tell, hopped from the back of his wretched saddle and onto his head and suddenly seemed to become very much alive. If he were able now to behold his reflection in a mirror and observe the patchwork hash of which his finely groomed hair had been made, he would probably be unable to refrain from weeping, since, as with all the Bikki, his hair had been his pride and joy. "Poor, poor Bikki Number Four," he would likely have cried, or something equally eloquent in its pity.

I know for certain, however, that he did not, in fact, have a mirror in his possession, so instead of weeping he was seething with anger. This wretched bird had knocked him off his horse, and the wretched horse had promptly run away—this despite the fact that the wretched messenger who had accompanied him had managed to retrieve his own horse without too much trouble. It was colossally, magnificently, unjust. Wretchedly unfair. What's more, he had fallen into the snow and the snow was wet, and a good deal of that wetness had been transferred to the Bikki's clothes and left the Bikki himself wet. He hated being wet. All of it—all—was the fault of this miserable, wretched, wretched, miserable bird.

No sooner had the (damp) Bikki Number Four dispatched the messenger to the king with a new and decidedly unpleasant message, to wit, "Wretched bird has escaped and run off into wretched forest south of Trondheim," when he turned and made his way into the wretched forest wherein that wretched bird had disappeared. Oh yes, he would find him. He wasn't about to be made a fool of by an unfeathered bird, no matter how afraid he'd been of it before. He was going to find it and he was going to wring its neck like some plucked chicken preparing for the pot!

So now he was tramping through the snow of the forest, without benefit of the snowshoes that had been tied to the saddle of his wretched runaway horse. His belly was grumbling for the lack of the dinner that had also been tied there, and it was just beginning to dawn on Bikki Number Four that he should have booted the messenger off his horse and taken it for himself, when suddenly he spotted his quarry through the trees.

The falcon was having what looked very much like a private conversation with a little girl as the two of them peered down at something in the snow. It gave Bikki Number Four pause somewhat, to see that the falcon was unhooded and had therefore become an even more formidable opponent. A little ways away from them was a creature that gave him further pause, since it appeared to be an enormous man, ten feet or more in height. But then he noted with great relief that the giant was clearly asleep. Bikki Number Four wagered he could accomplish his business in a few moments and be on his way without being troubled by any wretched sleeping giant, and certainly not by some wretched little girl. He crept his way closer and crawled into some bushes that lay between himself and the clearing where the pair was crouching over their oh-so-fascinating little patch of snow. He drew his dagger, took a deep breath, and then, in a moment, was upon them.

"Try to shame me, will you?" he shrieked. "You're just a plucked pheasant preparing for the feasting tables!"

What happened next he was decidedly unprepared for, since he was never prepared for anything, really. The truth is, I have a little bit of affection for this fellow. Perhaps you can tell. I don't know why. Except that, despite all his efforts to the contrary, he won't be hurting a soul in this story. Neither this nor any other. This I say because I can.

Case in point: in this moment, before Bikki Number Four even had a chance to thrust his dagger, he found that the wretched falcon was upon him—upon his head, to be exact—and once again tearing his hair out in tufts the size of rabbits' tails. The dagger had somehow been knocked from his grip and in its place there was a small talon-slash that smarted something terrible. It might have given him some satisfaction to see that the great ten-foot layabout he'd earlier noticed had jumped to his feet and run off into the forest. There was no time for such satisfaction, however, as the next thing he knew he was down on the ground and the falcon was hopping up and down on his chest, jabbering in his face. The snow was so deep that he couldn't get up easily, and he could feel again the seeping wetness creeping up through the canvas weave of his pants. He shrieked with rage and tried to clutch at the jabbering bird, but the falcon leapt up in the air, turned swiftly on its ragged tail and was gone. The little girl had taken off running through the forest and the bird was skittering after her. Bikki Number Four was panting hard from all his terrible trials, but he had become so enraged that with all the breath left in his lungs he howled after the wretched new master of this wretched falcon:

"My bottom is wet and you will pay for it! Don't think you won't! I have already sent a message to King Erik, and even now I am certain that the Blood-Axed one will have already set out to hunt you down. When he catches you, it won't matter the least little bit that you are just a dainty precious little girl. You are a thief! A wretched little thief! And for that he will most probably lock you away in his deep, dark, old, dead oak tree-trunk prison! Do you hear me? King Erik Blood-Axe will hunt you down and throw you with the greatest satisfaction into the coldest and most terrible gaol!"

They were almost out of earshot and he was not nearly finished howling at them yet, and so with what he himself considered to be a heroic burst of effort, Bikki Number Four scrambled to his feet and set off after them as fast as he could run. His mettle was being tested now, and he was determined to be the mettlest

Bikki of them all, punisher of falcons and runaway horses and outlaw children. Of his bold undertaking in the forest of Trondheim, the king's poets would surely sing. He was prepared now to pursue them beyond the ends of the earth, and was just about to redouble his speed when an enormous shadow suddenly rose up in front of him, stopping him short.

Rearing up in front of him was a black horse that seemed to have appeared out of thin air, frothing and blowing and lashing with its front hooves. It terrified him. He fell once again into the snow as the front hooves came down inches away from his legs. "I shall be trampled!" he cried, despite himself. And then he looked up. Astride the fearful beast was a woman clad all in armour, with black flowing hair and blazing eyes. Above her head, she had raised an enormous broadsword, and it seemed very much like she was going to hurl it straight down into his breast. Still higher above her head, he saw the most terrifying thing of all: a pair of enormous, bejewelled wings, containing stars, with tips as sharp as blades, spreading everywhere from her shoulders, blocking the tops of trees and filling the whole grey sky above the Bikki's upturned face. Such a sight he had never seen before in all his Bikki-born days, and he would never forget it either for as long as he lived, though it was true he would come to live a long, long time—longer than you can possibly imagine. Again the stallion reared, its eyes rolling up into its head, and when the beast came down again the woman gave a piercing cry and swung the sword down and around so that it whirred a mere inch or two in front of his nose.

With twice the energy and speed by which he earlier felt he could overtake falcons and children, Bikki Number Four turned tail, barely even bothering to jump to his feet, and ran. He ran through the clearing and into the trees, sending up great powdery billows as he went. He ran without looking back and soon broke from the edge of the forest. He didn't stop running then but kept on, long into the afternoon. He ran with a wet bottom and he was still running when his bottom dried. He ran and ran and ran and ran. If he were to have beheld himself in a mirror as he ran—if that were even possible—and if he had the time to feel surprise at what he beheld, he would have been surprised to see that the few patches of hair he had left on his bloodied hash of a head had turned entirely to white.

A Falcon's Wisdom

FREYA RAN THROUGH the forest until she was quite out of breath. She was terrified and confused and angry all at once. The thought that Freya the Falcon-Catcher, honoured servant of the king, should be so suddenly and swiftly transformed into Freya the Outlaw, destined to be hunted down and locked away in a deep, dark, old, dead oak tree-trunk prison, was overwhelming to her. She tripped over roots and ran into trees and got scuffed and scratched and kept right on running. She broke through a patch of particularly dense brush, getting a face full of snow, and then ploughed straight into Rolf, who was leaning and panting against a tall tree. Her brother yelped with fear and took off again. "Rolf!" she cried, and he came to a stop just as the falcon cleared the bush behind and barrelled into her. For the second time that day she was knocked off her feet and sent tumbling in the embrace of this great bony bird. When they came to a stop, Freya and the falcon lay panting side by side in the dirt, gazing up at the tops of the trees. They were in a small, dimly lit clearing, so tightly enclosed that no snow had fallen there, and Freya felt the pine needles in her hair. They lay silently for a few moments until finally the falcon spoke.

"So it's done then," he said with a strange, maddening note of cheer. "You will be my falconer."

Freya was overtaken by such a wave of helplessness and despair that she thought she was going to die. Tears rolled out of her eyes and down her cheeks. Really, she thought, if she was now considered a criminal, it was all the fault of this big, stupid bird and his wily ways. Meanwhile, to add insult to injury, she could see Rolf perched warily, uselessly, at the other edge of the clearing, ready at any moment to bound off again into the bush. When it came right down to it, she was all alone. So alone, in fact, that she might as well already be sitting in the deep, dark, old, dead oak tree-trunk prison.

Or so she felt, and when she spoke her voice was full of mourning for her own life. "I am an outlaw. . . . And soon the night will fall. . . . Outlaws have to tramp about at night. . . . " She wasn't speaking to anyone in particular. "My father will soon put the goats to bed. He'll wonder where I am. Maybe he'll shed a tear or two for me before dropping off to sleep."

"Don't be afraid, young girl," said the falcon in his gentlest voice. "I will stick by you."

"Oh, so what?" Freya muttered bitterly, half to herself. "You're a falcon that can't even fly."

"Now, now," said Morton, still gently. "You don't want to be unkind. I may have no wings, but I still managed to protect you from the clutches of the Bikki."

"What's a Bikki?" she was going to ask, petulantly, but the falcon went on.

"It's just as those rabbit tracks foretold. That you and I would be ambushed and yet we would stick together and win the day."

Morton's words burst the large dam that had been welling inside the little Freya. "Oh, thank you so much! Thanks ever so much! I never would have gotten into his clutches in the first place if it hadn't been for you! Why did you even have to run after me? Why didn't you run off in some other direction? Why didn't you just go set yourself free? That man thinks I'm your keeper! He wouldn't even be chasing after me now if I'd had the chance to just explain how I meant to serve the king, how I meant to be a great falcon-catcher on his behalf, how I meant to return his big, ugly, useless, ragged falcon to him!"

She was weeping again, sobbing into her sleeve. It would perhaps have been a heart-wrenching sight for anyone sitting by her, but human faces are as unreadable to falcons as falcon faces are to humans, so Morton merely continued the conversation. "Then why didn't you?" he asked.

"Why didn't I what?" asked the angry, sobbing Freya.

"Why didn't you explain that you were Freya the Falcon-Catcher, trying to catch a falcon for the king? Why didn't you return me to him?"

"You know very well there was no time, you stupid bird! You were fighting and I was running and he was just about the scariest—"

"Let's go back," said Morton, still calmly. "It's not too late."

Freya sat and sobbed a little more, ignoring this impossible bird.

"Return and hand me over to him," said the falcon.

"I can't do that," said Freya, suddenly stopping and wiping away her tears.

"Why not?" asked Morton.

"Because you wouldn't let me," said Freya, huffily.

"Yes, I would."

"You won't go back freely."

"I will."

"No you won't."

"I'm telling you, I will go back, right now," he declared, evenly.

Freya paused for a moment to consider, and then shook her head. "It's too late."

"It's not," he said.

"Would you shut up!" she shouted suddenly. "It is so! He would kill us all!"

"No, he would not. You could bargain with him. I will tell you exactly how to do it. Stand in the trees at a safe distance and say that you will hand me over in return for safe passage. What's more, you could tell him that you will never, ever breathe a word about his ineptness and bungling in his task, that you will never, ever reveal to anyone that he allowed himself to be defeated by ..." here Morton paused for emphasis before continuing, "... to be defeated by a ragged, ugly, useless falcon and a young girl. Negotiate with him like that and he will surely accept your terms. And then all you have to do is hand me over."

Freya was looking at Morton with skeptical disbelief, but she was no longer crying. "You would never let me do that," she said.

"I would," said the falcon.

"Well, I can't do that. How could I do that? It's silly and it's ... it's unfair. Completely unfair. You know very well I can't do that."

"So then it is you who has chosen to stick by me," said Morton quietly. "Brave girl."

Freya could not believe her ears. The last thing she expected or wished for was to hear praise from this bird that had gotten her into so much trouble. It frightened her, almost beyond measure. It hit her with a great burden of responsibility that she could barely even understand, but which was causing her to feel really very much alone in a fast-growing world.

"I am not a brave girl!" she shouted. "I am not a brave girl! Shut up!" Then she jumped to her feet and ran over to the still-cowering Rolf. She stopped short of swatting him in the shins but shouted nonetheless, making sure that she was speaking so clearly in their human language that even a great oaf of a brother would be sure to understand.

"And you ran away, Rolf, you coward! Can't you see how you could have swatted that man right over the trees? Have you no courage?"

"You shouldn't talk to him like that," said the bird. "He's just a young—"

"Stay out of this, plucked one," said Freya, turning to interrupt the bird, but Morton went straight on.

"He is clearly just a young boy. Any fool can see that. Even a bird can see that. What is his name?"

Freya was usually quite comfortable being rude, and she really would have preferred not to answer the falcon, but there was something so warm about his tone—almost paternal, beyond anything that might have been mustered lately by her father, and certainly protective of Rolf—that she felt suddenly quite a bit more rude than she felt a human should be, really, when it comes right down to it, when being addressed by a member of a whole entirely different species.

"His name is Rolf, Rolf the Ranger," she said finally, somewhat huffily. "So called because he's grown so big that he can't ride a horse and has to walk everywhere on foot."

"I see," said the falcon. "Those who so called him were correct: he is big. He is very big indeed."

Rolf could see that his sister and the bird had taken

up their squawking and twittering again, but this time he had the uncanny impression that the subject of all their squawking and twittering was none other than him. The falcon had, in fact, hopped a few steps closer, and, if Rolf wasn't entirely mistaken, (and he felt he probably was), had just winked at him.

"Let me tell you something about your little big brother," said the falcon, sizing up Rolf with some approval, "or rather your big little brother. This brother of yours is a true giant, such as we northern creatures have not actually seen in several hundred years. The poets of old wrote tales of them in an ancient book called the Edda, which I mentioned to you before. This same book is the only one to have come down to us that tells how things used to be in those days, when the gods and the giants and even the Valkyries roamed the North and were very common around these parts. It is also quite possibly the only book in the history of the world that has been translated into virtually all the tongues of the northern creatures. There's only one copy of each, mind you, and to read the falcon version you have to fly across the ocean to Iceland, where someone has pecked the runes into a large flat stone. It is said in the Edda that the race of giants are the oldest and wisest inhabitants of the universe. I'll bet you did not know that, did you?"

"Pah," said Freya, who didn't believe in such stories and said so. "My brother is neither old nor wise," she declared. "He's just a great big cowardly oaf. That's the whole truth of the matter."

"He is a child, it's true," said the falcon. "But there is no use in rebuking a child for having childish ways. It is still a fact, if the evidence of my eyes can be believed, that your brother is a giant. And since he is a giant, that means he is also part of a great mystery. You see, the Edda tells how giants had prodigious memories of all things past, and great strength; that they were there at the beginning of time, before the gods even, but that they became sworn enemies of the gods. It was the war between the giants and the gods that was to bring about the end of the world for gods and giants both—a great battle called Ragnarök. Some say that end has happened, and that is why there are no giants anymore. Others say it has not happened, and that giants are merely secretive and elusive beings."

Freya found herself wishing that Rolf was a more elusive being and that the hawk wouldn't talk about him so much. Now he was talking nonsense about a war that was in the past or the future and didn't make any sense. Ragnarök. She wondered for a moment whether Ragnarök was a war the likes of which the world had never seen. Whether it had been a battle like the one her father had witnessed. Still, her father could not have meant Ragnarök. Ragnarök was the end of the world and the world was still here. There was proof. Freya was standing in it.

Still, her head was spinning. And there was another galling, burning, nagging question: if Rolf was a giant, then why wasn't she? They were brother and sister. So why were she and Rolf so different?

Morton was waiting patiently. He knew he had given Freya much to think about, and so he watched her stand and mull and look at the sky. Finally, she looked at him again and he said, cheerfully, "I wonder if you would do me the kindness of telling your brother something for me."

"Me?" said Freya.

"There's nobody else here who can translate my tongue into yours, is there? If you will not tell him what I have to say then nobody will, and that would be a shame. For these words will be very useful for him to hear. They concern this matter of cowardice—the feeling of fear in the face of danger and adversity."

"Oh, very well," said Freya. "Tell me what it is that you want to say to him, and then I'll decide whether or not I will translate."

"Good enough," said the bird. "Tell him for me that he should hold his head high. Tell him what I said before about the wisdom of the race of giants. Tell him that if he has been born a giant then—"

"Wait!" cried Freya. "I won't be able to remember all that; give me a chance to get started."

"But you just said—"

"It doesn't matter what I said!" shouted Freya, who felt she had the right to be cross since she was undertaking this favour to benefit this bird and her brother, but not getting anything out of it herself. "Let me just get started and then I'll tell you when you can carry on with your oh-so-important advice."

And then Freya turned to Rolf and, with the sense that there had never been a task created in the whole history of the world that was stupider than this one, explained to him everything the falcon had told her about the race of giants being old and wise, and the battle with the gods and blather blather bother blather bother.

"I'm not saying you should believe all of this," she added, though her tone suggested in fact that he should believe exactly none of it. "It's just what the old bird told me to tell you and so I'm telling you and so there now, you're told."

Rolf, for his part—and despite all his sister's efforts—was about as impressed as a boy who's just been told he's from an ancient and mysterious race could possibly be. He dropped down onto his knees and looked more closely at the falcon who suddenly didn't seem to scare him anymore. Freya was more than a little annoyed by all this, and hoped that the undue attention being paid to a big stupid oaf of a brother would end very soon.

"There, I'm all caught up," she said to the falcon. "Go on if you really must."

"Thank you, brave and noble girl," said Morton, causing Freya to stamp her foot and roll her eyes. "Tell him that if he has been born a giant, then there must be some purpose in the world for him. Giants don't just get put here for nothing, you know. Tell him that next time he's in a tight spot and feeling a little uncertain, he should just say to himself, 'I'm a giant. I'll get myself out of this.'"

"Oh, brother," said Freya. "And will that be all? After that I'll be done?"

"Yes," said the falcon. "After that, you'll be done."

"Very well," said Freya, and then she did what she was told and passed the message on to Rolf. When she finished, she saw a mixture of awe and pride on her brother's face. She felt equally gratified and annoyed by this, and the mixture of these two feelings confused her. She saw her brother's eyes well up with tears and, despite herself, she felt one or two tears squeeze forth from her own eyes as well. Such noble ideas had never been expressed to these children before. She suddenly felt that everything she had said about becoming a great falcon-catcher seemed just so much empty boasting. Suddenly, the grey sky above and the bare trees all around lost a little bit of their dullness and presented themselves as a land that she knew well and loved. Just like her brother. Her stupid oaf of a brother. Her big stupid oaf of an only brother. Her own big stupid oaf of an only brother. She felt a sudden warmth inside her that she hadn't felt since before the snow came, and before Rolf grew, and this warmth itself grew into the thought that this forest and this sky were, in spite of all their flaws and disappointments, her home. And this brother was, for all his flaws and disappointments, her own and only brother. These were the thoughts that sprang unbidden to Freya's mind as she caught the shining wet eyes of Rolf, and then looked away.

"There," she said flatly to the bird. "Everything you've said has been said." She observed him warily from the corner of her eye, trying not to betray the unfamiliar feeling that his well-spoken words had engendered in her.

"Thank you," said Morton. "And as for you, brave Freya the Falcon-Catcher, perhaps you've had enough battles and broils for one afternoon. If you allow me to, I shall lead you home to your goatherd father, and then he will no longer be worried. And then I will go and present myself before the king so that, by the will of Odin, he will leave you alone."

Freya's eyes grew wide and she looked at the falcon, who now seemed himself to have transformed. He bore the appearance of a kind of tall and shattered prince, who had lost none of his dignity despite his troubles; who had, in fact, grown in stature by them.

"You..." she ventured, who had rarely in her whole life left a sentence unfinished. "So you want to...you wish to return to the king?"

"Well," said the falcon, "night will soon fall. A falcon should not be out at all at night when the world itself is hooded and still."

"But, but," said Freya, "but you can get around in the dark, you've proved that. You can get around with a blindfold on, which is the same as being in the dark — worse, in fact, much worse. That hood must have made a darkness that no night could ever . . . could ever . . ."

"I have no home," said the falcon. "The longhouse of the king is the only home I have ever known. And I miss my civil conversations with the sparrows that make their homes underneath the eaves."

"But how will you explain yourself to the king? Even if there was something you could say, how would you say it? If he does not understand the language of birds? How will you—"

"I will find a way," said Morton, turning his tattered back to her and looking toward the south. "My appearance will make things very clear."

Freya understood one thing with much clarity, with stubborn certainty, in fact: this falcon's fate had become tied to hers, from the moment he had run into her net. She had blamed him for her troubles, but really it was she who had set a trap for him and she who had caught him in that trap. He had come to her through no fault of his own, and now he was trying to sacrifice himself in order to save her.

"But he will kill you," she said.

"Perhaps not," said the falcon. "Perhaps he will only send me again to his brother."

"Then he will kill you," she said, still with stubborn certainty.

"Perhaps not," said the falcon.

"He will," said Freya. "He will. And you won't even be able to fly away and make your escape. King Erik must be an evil king."

"He is a warrior," said Morton. "His heart is as hard as his head."

"My father once told me," said Freya, surprised by the memory, "that a dragonfly's heart is in his wings. If that's true, then the wings of a falcon must hold his heart and soul and strength and spirit and all. You cannot be denied that. You must get the chance to fly again. You must soar the skies above the clouds, and see the sun, and be a creature of light and shade all the days of your life."

Now Freya's voice became heated, and she was almost shouting, having utterly given in to this unfamiliar state of mind.

"Even a kept bird—a hunting bird with a keeper— is allowed the chance to fly! There is no justice in a kingdom in which the king would pull the feathers from his own bird!"

She went on, her voice rising to a fever pitch, containing all the disappointment she had held inside through the long winter of her father's gloom, her brother's changing youth, her own desperate loneliness—all funnelled together into this moment of anger and empathy for a flight-torn falcon.

"It's unjust! I am angry! That my country should have such a king!"

She stood up as tall as she could and shouted at the sky, "I AM ANGRY!"

And then, as her cry echoed past the tops of the trees, she was surprised to hear an answer that was more than an echo. Shrill and high, she heard her

words return again to her, "I am angry!" And then
again, "Angry!" And just as she was beginning to
believe that it really was just an echo after all, she
heard a new sound: a high, piercing battle cry. It was
the voice of a woman and it was answered by another,
equally strong and high. And then, as she looked to
Rolf and the falcon and found that they, too, had heard
all this, there came the sound of sudden thundering
hooves, and then another cry and another answer, and
the hooves were getting louder, approaching them.
Two enormous black shapes were galloping through
the trees toward them. Freya thought they were about
to break into the full view of the clearing, but at the last
minute they veered and parted ways, flanking them as
they rode by, but keeping at such a distance that she
could not say for certain who or what they were.
Through the shadows of the trees Freya could make
out the sheen of sweat on the horses' black hides, the
flash of upraised swords, and something else—a glimmer
like a shaft of sunlight that pierced their shoulders.
Were they wings? In the shadows and the distance it
was impossible to say. All that was certain to Freya
was the feeling that the sun had broken through the
clouds for a moment of headlong blazing—like a fire
that would burn everything—and that something had
ridden by, straight out of her dreams.

And then they were gone, leaping over bushes and
disappearing through spaces between trees that seemed
far too narrow to contain their enormous forms.

"Oh . . . ," said Freya. "I . . . I wonder if . . . I wonder if we . . . disturbed them somehow . . . or maybe they. . . ."

The falcon was looking very directly at her, peering at her more intensely than he had before. "They shouted your anger with you, and raised their arms as they went by," he said. "Who are they? Do you know them?"

"I . . . I . . . ," said Freya, who only just now noticed that Rolf had not cowered through the ordeal but indeed was standing close to them in the middle of the clearing. Could he have been seeking to protect her? Freya wondered to herself. It seemed unlikely and she dismissed the thought.

"Well, go on," urged the falcon. "Do you know them?"

"I. . . ." Freya wondered whether she should say that she had sometimes seen these figures, or figures like them, since the days she had first wandered into the forest, riding almost beyond the edge of her sight. But her memory was playing tricks on her, since in her mind's eye it was not now Freya herself who was looking toward the horizon with its vanishing riders, but rather her father. Turning from the horizon to speak to Freya, his face both smiling and serious, he's telling her something; a newfound bit of broken rune stone in his hand, Freya herself no more than six years old. He has walked with her some distance into the wood. They've brought a small bundle of carrots with them for lunch; the goats have all, somehow, stayed behind. He is pointing now to the north and saying, "You know, Freya, our country becomes nothing more than a sliver of land as it travels to the north from here, a sliver between the ocean and the continent. But such a sliver is enough space for a trail to take the finest horse from the furthest northernmost point, straight to our door. One day such a horse will come, you'll see."

Mysterious words like that, half forgotten till now, eventually replaced by the later, more recent image of her father, his eyes fixed, his bitter gloom. And those figures in the woods—they had never come, they had never ridden so close as this before. It was unlikely that these were even the same ones, and anyway it was likely the falcon would not believe her.

Freya blinked. Morton was waiting patiently. She shook her head. No, she did not know them. The falcon cocked his head and she thought she caught a glimpse of skepticism in his eyes. "What are they?" she said, although she thought she had said, "Who are they?" which is what she had meant to say.

The falcon fixed her with yet another unfamiliar look, and his dull golden eyes seemed to shine with new polish. "They are Valkyries," he said.

"They?" Freya was overcome with awe. "They are Valkyries?"

"I am certain of it," said the bird. "It is often said that Valkyries are creatures of evil and injustice, choosers of the slain on the battlefield. But did you see how they called out their alliance with you? They shouted your anger and raised their weapons to you as they rode by. Whatever cause you have chosen to shout forth seems to be, in their eyes, a just cause. Though they have long been known to terrify warriors on the battlefield, it has always been plain to the birds of the air that these women choose to be allies of the just campaign, that they soar above the battlefields and anyone who dies valiantly is taken by them to the great feasting halls of Odin and the gods, where they sit and feast and tell stories, and drink from horns of victory with other brave Viking warriors."

"But . . . ," Freya was full of questions. "But where do they come from?"

"These creatures fall halfway between the world of the gods and the world of men. Many have at least one human parent."

"But they have great wings," countered the awed and puzzled Freya. She could not quite believe her ears. "Humans can't have wings . . . can they?"

The falcon seemed now to be smiling at her, though how a bird could be perceived to smile it is impossible to say. She was perhaps imagining it. All of a sudden the threat of the Bikki seemed very far away.

"You are young," said the falcon to the girl. "Just like your brother. There are many wonders in the world that you have yet to see."

"Yes, but a human with wings?"

"Valkyries aren't born with them, you know. There comes a time in their young lives, however, when such things sprout from their shoulders, like flowers in spring."

"Really?" said Freya. "Like flowers in spring?"

"Exactly," said the bird. "But far more useful."

Freya turned to Rolf, who was standing at his full height before her. She remembered what the falcon had said about her brother becoming wise and strong and brave like the giants who had once been the envy of all the gods. It seemed possible to her suddenly. "Rolf!" she cried, "What if I suddenly had wings? If I had wings, I could keep up with you when you go ranging through the forest! I could fly above your head, above the trees, above the clouds! If I had wings, I could seek out stray goats for Father and find new feeding grounds for him!"

And then Freya turned again and regarded the bird hunched there in the snow beside her giant brother. He had become to her the most beautiful creature she had ever seen, emanating wisdom and mystery from every tattered feather and exposed bone. "You have told us so much already," she said. "But there is still one thing I don't know. What is your name? Have you got a name?"

"Yes, I have a name," said the falcon. "And through some miracle it is the same in the human as in the falcon tongue. My name is Morton."

"Morton," she said. And then again. "Morton."

"It's a funny name, I know," said Morton. "More like a name for a scrivener or a merchant than a hunting hawk."

"I don't think it's a funny name at all!" shouted Freya, in her bossiest manner. And then she turned and spoke more softly to her brother. "Rolf, this falcon is our friend, and his name is Morton."

Rolf nodded his head.

"And Rolf, I am sorry for having left you so completely in the dark. All this time you've been watching me jabber away at Morton, for hours on end. And then to get chased by some terrible man, and then to see these two women ride by on horseback, and not get the benefit of an explanation about any of it! Not that I have much of an explanation, but still. You must be mystified, Rolf! You must be so completely mystified!"

Rolf shrugged and then nodded his head.

"Well, there, I apologize Rolf. I hope that'll do. And I'll fill you in."

"Yes," said Rolf. "In." He was openly weeping now at his sister's deep and sudden overflow of kindness. Tears rolled down his cheeks the size of chestnuts, though everyone did their best to ignore them.

"Very well," continued Freya, trying not to weep herself. "This falcon, our friend named Morton, has lost his wings. They were torn from him by a terrible king, the very same king that you and I were planning to serve, in fact. But that king is not a just king, Rolf. He is a nasty, horrible king and he must be made to give up these same stolen wings. Our friend Morton must soar again the skies above the clouds, see the sun and be a creature of light and shade all the days of his life!"

There are some things, Morton was thinking quietly to himself, that a creature cannot put back together once they have been torn apart. Still, he was moved by the young girl's conviction, and he thought that something good was bound to come of this, as he observed her continue to inform and inspire her brother.

"Stand up straight, Rolf! Hold your ground! We said that we would one day go and behold the king of Norway, and today is the day that we are going! Or rather tomorrow, since the shadows are growing long and we must get a good night's sleep before we embark. The three of us should be enough to right this wrong, so long as we have fire in our hearts and justice in our minds! What do you think of that, Rolf?"

"Yes!" shouted the ecstatic Rolf, standing as tall as he could, wishing and worried that he might be asked to prove that he could be wise and brave and strong and a giant and one of the oldest inhabitants of the universe. And then he shouted again, as loud as he could, "Return the wings to Morton the bird, friend to Freya and Rolf!" Twelve words he uttered—more than he had ever spoken before in a single sentence. And then he blushed, having said something so simple and clear.

You may ask why should Freya, who so far has been bratty and petulant and stubborn and rude and disrespectful and selfish, suddenly become brave and somewhat noble and even considerate of her brother's feelings? Could it be because she needs his help and has recognized that he is capable of powers that she has never before acknowledged? Perhaps that is selfish, but we must also ask ourselves, what is the nature of this help she so seemingly selfishly seeks from him? Why should she choose to embark, against terrible odds, on a campaign to retrieve the feathers of her new friend the falcon? Why should she choose to go and face a king who has proven himself to be a cruel king, who would very likely care nothing about the wishes of a little girl? It might be the thought that there is something inside her, something that has been recognized and identified by her newfound unfeathered friend, this tattered bird. Something that makes her feel large within herself. He has called her brave, and this alone perhaps has caused powerful wings to spring from a hidden place within her heart to take the place of the ones he has lost. And along with the thought that there is nothing like a new language to open up a new window upon the world, although this language is one she could only have learned in her nightly dreams, still these things are enough I think to transform a bratty, petulant, stubborn, rude, disrespectful, and selfish little girl into something very much the opposite of that: the hero of this story.

13

Bikki Number O

BIKKI NUMBER FOUR was still running.
He'd long since forgotten that his bottom had
ever bothered him by being wet, though he
had fallen several more times in the snow and gotten
wet in far more places than his bottom. He had just
about run himself out, so tired was he that he could feel
his bones grinding together inside his skin. So when he
stumbled over the snowy crest of a certain hill and saw
the Viking army of Erik Blood-Axe heading toward
him from the darkening south, the joy that filled his
heart made him all but forget that his had been a failed
mission and that he was going to have to answer for it.
He had thus far sustained himself with the thought
that he was bringing news of the strange creatures he
had seen in the woods, whose beauty and terror were

fit only to be described to the king.

For his part, the tired Erik Blood-Axe rode slowly at the head of an army of some two hundred men, all trudging in their heavy Viking armour through the gathering grey of a sunless dusk. In front of the king walked his standard-bearer, who carefully balanced a tall staff in his two hands. At the top of the staff, in place of the usual standard, hung the splayed span of Morton's feathers. Though they had been torn from his wings and back, they had strangely retained the shape of a wingspan, and dangled above the army like a feathered corpse, a banner of war and of fear.

Just behind the king rode the other three Bikki, all sitting high and proud on their horses. They were prouder than usual, really, I suppose on account of the fact that they were now a group of three, and the idea of three seemed far more exclusive to them than four. Since all three of them had come privately and separately to this conclusion, it had privately and separately occurred to each of them as well that if the number could be reduced to one—one single Bikki—then that would be the most exclusive state of all, and the number which appended each of their names could be permanently removed. It must be said, in addition, that each of these Bikki thought of himself not only as an individual, but also as the individual most deserving of this exclusive singularity. How strange it is then to note that each of these three alleged individuals should happen to be having the exact same collection of thoughts, appearing in his mind in precisely the same order as it did in the minds of his fellows. As they rode behind the king, they glanced furtively at one another, wondering what the coming promise of war held in store for them.

"Ah!" said Erik Blood-Axe, as he rode. "Look there. If it isn't Bikki Number Four, returning like a sheep to the fold."

Bikki Number Four did not know it yet, but he had been tried in his absence and found guilty of botching up an affair of state. His sentence, it goes without saying, was death. This same sentence had been bestowed upon the messenger when he had come earlier upon the Viking army on its march toward the North. The messenger's fine and beautiful horse was now being ridden proudly by Bikki Number Three. As Bikki Number Four stumbled down the hill toward the king, it should perhaps have occurred to him that he was in serious trouble, but it must be said about Bikki Number Four that he was a loyal servant, though his loyalty was in the service of a tyrant. It should also be noted in his favour that, for the first time in the many years spent in their company, Bikki Number Four had, at this moment, an entirely different set of thoughts running through his mind than his fellow more favoured Bikki, and he was feeling a great desire to share these thoughts with his king. He stumbled at last into earshot and began to shout in the general direction of the army. He was so exhausted that his words came out in short bursts.

"Sire!" he cried. "Women! Horses! Wings! Swords

and fire! Drove away!"

Then he stopped short with a sudden realization, and slapped his forehead, finally getting a complete picture in his mind of what it was he had actually seen.

"Valkyries!" he cried. "Warrior women with wings! Valkyries!"

Like many a northern child before him, Bikki Number Four had long ago been told stories by his mother about the terrible Valkyries who roamed the north on their horses and flew over the Viking battle-fields, choosing which warriors were to live and which were to die. He managed to recall these stories in this moment without actually recalling his mother, or himself as a child, since it does not befit a Viking warrior to conjure up memories of tenderness or love. Such stories, in fact, were told to frighten him in his bed and to try and discourage him from ever becoming a Viking warrior. His mother had hoped that he would rather choose to be a sheep farmer in the Oslo Shire. She would have been decidedly unhappy to witness her son the doomed henchman come at last to a halt before the horse of Erik Blood-Axe, Great King of Norway, where he spoke now with all the breath he had left inside himself.

"King Erik of Blood, there are Valkyries to the north! I have seen them, and by all evidence they seem to ride against us!"

"Hog dirt," declared Erik.

"Sire, I have seen them with my own eyes!"

"Not hog dirt that they are there or that you have

seen them; hog dirt that they ride against us. Did it occur to you, Bikki Number O, that they might, in fact, have been riding against you and you alone? For it is a well-known fact that the Choosers of the Slain cannot abide the sight of a coward and a bungler."

Bikki Number Four was shocked by this sudden charge, not to mention his sudden change in status, and, too late, a wave of fear came over him as Erik Blood-Axe turned to address his warriors.

"Do you hear what our former servant has told us? There are Valkyries waiting to welcome us to our battle-field in the North, ready to ride with us against the traitorous Tronds of Trondheim and their cowardly so-called sovereign. It is only natural that such pure Viking creatures would ride to the battle of a king so valiant, so proud as myself, whose reputation as a warrior is shouted to the heavens as high as the hall of Valhalla itself!"

King Erik Blood-Axe was not well-known for his modesty. He continued. "My brothers in blood! You must not fear these wild and winged sword-wielders but rather welcome them as a sign that our arms are strong and our will is supreme and shall be triumphant! A Valkyrie will recognize a coward as surely as that coward can see his own reflection in the glass. A Valkyrie does not choose for such a man to die, but rather allows him to live on in shame! Vikings! You and I were created for the field of battle! In the fight to come, some of us will be chosen for the honour of being carried from the field on the backs of such stout horses as these women ride! In the fight to come, some of us will be carried among the slain to the feasting tables of Odin, great god of all Vikings, where we will feast throughout eternity with all the valiant warriors who lived and fought in the days before us. Those who find their way to this fortune will be the lucky ones. The rest shall have to wait another day to reap their full reward of glory!"

Then he turned back to the pale and shivering Bikki Number Four, standing alone in front of the vast army, and addressed him.

"Bikki Number O, since it seems we will be joined in battle by such honourable creatures, I must perforce give you one last opportunity to complete your mission. It is through your bungling that my brother, Haakon the Good, has not yet been summoned to the battlefield. I have no wish to leap upon his shire unannounced. That would be the work of a coward. Since you yourself are a coward and therefore expendable to my army, I hereby spare you for a day and charge you to turn around and run back from whence you came. Do not be turned around by any Valkyrie on horseback, but make your way to my brother. You shall replace my plucked falcon in this task. Find Haakon by tomorrow morning. Tell him he is as fit to be king as your unfeathered self is fit to be the servant of a king. Tell him that tomorrow night I shall await his arrival on the Fields of Snorre, south of the forest of Trondheim. Go!"

The former Bikki Number Four turned to run. The

gathering gloom told him that he would have to run all through the darkness of night.

"Wait!" cried Erik, bringing the now-called Bikki Number O immediately to a halt. "I do not wish to see you run in that way."

Bikki trembled and said, "In what way, Your—?"

"In that way that you are running. Like a man, I mean. If you are going to be my featherless bird, you must be prepared to play the part. Flap your wings! Try to fly!"

For a moment, Bikki Number Four was past embarrassment. He regarded his king dully, seeing a whole lifetime of duty turn to dust before his eyes.

"Go on," said Erik Blood-Axe, King of Norway, almost kindly. And then he shouted. "Go on!"

Wheeling about on his feet, Bikki Number O took one tentative hop forward in the snow. He had, he thought, never been asked to play a role before. He raised his arms, poked his head forward in a (surprisingly well-observed, actually) imitation of Morton's stance, and started to run, skittering as best he could like the falcon he had seen run before him through field and forest. The blood now stood out on his face and tears streamed down his cheeks. No one stood close enough to hear him sob. From behind he could hear the laughter of the Vikings, and then again the shouting voice of King Erik.

"You're not yet good enough to be my messenger! Let's hear you squawk!"

"Ak!" cried Bikki as he ran. "Ak! Ak! Ak! Ak!" as he

flapped his arms and skittered through the snow. He ran up and over the crest of the hill and disappeared from Erik's sight. He could still hear the laughter echoing over the hill as he ran back in the direction of the forest and the falcon and the Valkyries and the little girl and the brother king. Sound travels farther in darkness, and so the laughter followed him farther than he expected or wished. His arms stayed aloft as he ran. No longer did he feel the grinding of his bones inside his skin. He was a bird now, at least in the eyes of his countrymen. His heart had been gripped by a bird's terror and his limbs had been gripped by a bird's vigour. He ran and skittered over twice-covered terrain, and sometimes as he ran his feet seemed to lift above the surface of the snow.

As he ran, a funny thing began to happen to Bikki Number O. For lack of a better model, he began to adopt many more of the characteristics of the falcon whom he had chased earlier on this longest of days. As he did this he began to realize, much to his own surprise, that he had noticed many details about that bird that had struck him as both funny and sad: the way it had skittered pathetically through the snow, blinded by its black hood. How difficult it must have been for it to run blinded like that! It recalled to him a time when he was a small child, before the Bikki days, when he had awoken in the middle of the night with his eyes fastened together from the goo of sleep, and he had been afraid, and his mother had taken a damp cloth from water heated over the fire and then coaxed his eyes open. It was, he thought as he ran, the first time in as long as he remembered that he had even thought of his mother, much less his own child self. And this thought led him to consider further another thought: that he had played a role before this one, since in fact Bikki Number Four, Servant to the King, was itself a role that he had had to fit into. It had nothing to do with him, with himself, the child of his mother who had opened his eyes with that damp cloth all those many years ago and he had looked up into her moon face glowing in the candlelight, as big as all the sky. As I have said before, sometimes it takes a terrible action to introduce a creature to himself. In the case of Bikki Number O, I can tell you that it is not merely a matter of speculation to say that this creature has been so introduced. I know it, for a fact, as if I were speaking of my very own self. (Though how, you may wonder, could I be speaking of my very own self if this story I tell you took place over a thousand years ago? You would be correct, really, to wonder.)

Now, as he ran, Bikki Number O remembered the exact way the falcon's wings had stuck out at odd angles from his body, the dismay and discomfort that bird must have felt at being reduced to such a state. Bikki Number O began to consider for the first time that this bird had not been deserving of its fate; that really, after all, it was just a bird, that birds are meant to possess the gift of flight, and how sad it was that this bird should lose such a gift. Bikki Number O began to realize that he had already felt a fondness and a sympathy for this bird, and that these feelings had not been acknowledged for the simple reason that they had not been useful to him. And now that he had begun to acknowledge such feelings as sympathy and fondness and the observation of insignificant details, Bikki Number O realized that he was losing his usefulness as a member of the collective Bikki. And so, as he ran and squawked and flapped his arms, Bikki Number O accomplished a very significant change within himself: his name. Admittedly, it wasn't much of a change, and if someone were to be reading this story out loud to you, you might not think that he changed anything at all. Still, for what it's worth, no longer was he Bikki Number Four or Bikki Number O or Bikki Number Anything. No longer was he even Bikki. This man, who skittered and squawked and ran toward the North, as the night began to fall all around him, had given himself a brand new name, and it was The Beaky, or simply Beaky, the one and only.

Night

FREYA LAY AWAKE in the hay. Beside her, Rolf's great chest heaved up and down in the unmistakable rhythm of sleep, causing small rustling sounds in the hay. The falcon perched nearby, in the nook of a long beam that secured the wall of the second-storey loft to the roof of the barn. The three of them had decided to sleep in Freya's father's hayloft, so they could get a good night's sleep before the next day's great adventures without involving anyone else in their pact. Their father would likely have laid aside his gloomy preoccupations and asked too many questions, and he would have been afraid of the falcon on behalf of his goats. The goats, for their part, rested safely in the barn below, without the smallest awareness of the raptor that slept a few feet above their heads. Freya alone lay awake, since there was much that occupied her mind from this longest and richest of days that had just ended. She felt she was caught up in a series of events whose conclusions would answer many questions for her. Would Morton fly again? Would she be able to speak bravely to the cruel tyrant king? Would she be able to protect her younger brother Rolf in all this? Most important of all, would the women on horseback appear once again to feed her courage? And would they stay long enough that she might speak to them? And would they speak back to her and tell her who they were and where they came from?

And, surfacing unexpectedly among all these thoughts and questions was another question: the question of her own unknown mother. This came as a great surprise to Freya since this was the first time she had thought of her mother in many years. As she lay there in the dark, she spoke the word out loud that had been banished from her mind in the reflected face of her father's sadness in the glass.

"Mother."

Who was her mother? Why had her father never spoken of her? Once, Freya had heard him hurriedly explain to Rolf that she had died when Freya and Rolf were very young. But if she had been with them up until the birth of Rolf, then why did Freya have no memory of her at all? Why did it seem to her, in fact, that she and her father had been alone before Rolf came along, and that one day a long, long time ago—

before the days in her life that she remembered easily —
an infant had appeared, and her father had said that
this was her brother? She suddenly remembered this
day distinctly, though it seemed to have just sprung
from a trap door in her memory where she had never
known to look before. Now she prodded further and
remembered new things, further things. The talk of
children in the village; taunts and lies to account for a
missing mother; that the villagers of Trondheim had
somehow disapproved of her father's wife; that they
had considered her to be an evil woman — that was the
word the taunting children had used, "evil" — and in the
stories they told it was said that the villagers had driven
her out. Freya had always known that she had never
much sought the company of other children, but she had
never before now considered that there had actually been
a reason why. She recalled that she had been considered
a strange child, the daughter of a strange man. She
recalled that she had, in fact, been shunned more than
once from the company of children whom she thought
she had loved, whom she had thought to be her best
friends, and had long since fallen back on the company
of her once tiny brother. She recalled the story oft told by
her father, wondering if the real memory was anywhere inside her, rather than just her father's telling of it:

"These people know nothing!"

"How can you prove that, Freya my daughter?"

"They prefer cows' milk to goats'!"

Freya lay in the dark and comfort of the hayloft,

listening to the occasional sound of the goats below and the breathing of her brother beside. She looked over and saw the shadow of the sleeping bird, nestled in the crook of the beam. She thought of her father, sleeping in the nearby house with its red painted door, and she imagined, not for the first time—though perhaps somewhat more clearly—the depth of his loneliness. Perhaps, she thought, her father had waited as long as he could endure for the woman he loved to return, riding the finest horse down the sliver of land from the north. Perhaps, she thought, his thoughts had turned from his children to his goats because the one he loved did not return and so that had been the end of the world for him. Perhaps he had lost her in a battle, the likes of which the world had never seen. Perhaps her father had silently longed for a wife as keenly as Freya had longed for a mother. Perhaps the loneliness of father and daughter had been the same.

And as Freya felt these new feelings and thought these new thoughts, the tears rolled silently down her cheeks. She touched them to see if they were gold or amber, but of course they were not. And just as her silent longing seemed to reach its summit, she fell soundlessly, unexpectedly, asleep.

Morton, for his part, only seemed to be asleep in the crook of the beam. He was, in fact, contemplating all the possible scenarios that might play themselves out when he and these two children wandered the next day into the middle of what could only be described as a civil war. The gods would see fit to punish anyone, he thought, who would willfully bring children into such a path of danger, and Morton did not wish to be so punished. Yet he was faced with a strong-willed young girl who was determined to face down this tyrant of a former master, and it seemed now to Morton that it was impossible for him to prevent her unless he was to resort to some of his craftier, wily, old bird ways. And so, with the teeming mind of the wisest and most clear-sighted general, he pondered everything that he knew. He flew over the whole of Norway in his mind and observed the principal players in this war as best he could with his mind's eye. It was a simple matter to conjure up a vision of Erik Blood-Axe, whom he knew well. But it was another matter altogether for him to conjure an image of Erik's brother and principal adver-sary. He had never seen this man, the declared king of Trondheim, before. The best he could do was soar on the wings of his memory back in time and contemplate the character and actions of the old master who had been father to both of these men. The old man had given his second son to Athelston, King of England, as a trick to fill the English king with fatherly affection and cause him to lay aside his warrior ways. The stratagem had worked, and now that little peacemaker child had grown up to become—what was it that the messenger had called him? Haakon. No, not just Haakon: Haakon the Good. And this second son, Haakon the Good, brother to Erik, had not sought to rule the Tronds of

Trondheim by force, but rather—according to the story of the messenger whom he had heard with his fine hawk hearing—the Tronds of Trondheim had requested that Haakon become their king. Haakon had been called to the role of leadership, and he had answered the call in spite of the danger that would come to him in the person of his own brother, Erik Blood-Axe.

Morton was no wizard. He could not unravel the future. Still, he had a choice at his disposal, and faced with the choice between allowing his small brave charge, one Freya the Falconer, to confront Erik Blood-Axe, King of all Norway and bearer of Morton's own bloody wingspan for his standard, or Haakon the Good, proclaimed King of Trondheim and foster son of England's wise King Athelston . . . faced with a choice between allowing his small new master to speak to the one or the other, Morton felt that his choice was eminently clear. Having made his decision, and listening to the peaceful breathing of the two children sleeping nearby, and ignoring as best he could the mouth-watering sounds of docile goats who rested below him, Morton drifted off to sleep.

Rolf, for his part, slept, and dreamt of wise giants climbing up into the tree of the world, and he was among them, and he was a giant too, ascending quietly and with a powerful grace into the expanding enormity of the tree. Up among the boughs and branches of the Tree of the World, there were many wonders. Life teemed there in all its insect and mammal and vegetable and gecko and fungal and avian glory. He saw birds he thought were flowers and lizards he thought were birds and flowers he thought were lizards and colours he had never seen before. A squirrel came and watched him for a long time, both in his dream and outside of it, in the darkness of the hayloft. And then his dream ended and he slept still deeper, he slept all the way till morning, preserving and replenishing his strength, so that when he woke he had long since forgotten his dream, though he felt very much refreshed and ready for the day ahead.

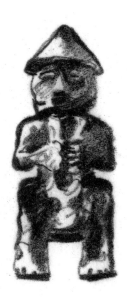

Morning

BACK IN THE FOREST the following morning, Freya and Morton were having an argument. Freya had declared that they should set off toward the South without expecting any debate, and in fact Rolf had wiped the sleep from his eyes and strode away in that direction with great conviction. But after striding for twenty or more paces he realized that his fellow travellers were not behind him. So he turned around and strode back, though with somewhat less conviction, and found Morton the falcon deep in thought, contemplating some deer track, or so it seemed, in the snow. Freya was stamping about impatiently.

"But why?" she shouted in the form of a question. "Why would we ever wish to head toward the North when we know for a fact that your feathers are with the king, and the king, according to all evidence that I can understand, is clearly in the South?"

"But I'm not sure," countered the thoughtful falcon. He had suddenly taken on a semblance of grave and irksome authority, at least according to Freya. "I'm not so sure that the king is still to the south of us, so I can only suggest that we proceed in a northward direction."

Rolf observed the falcon point a bony wingtip in the direction of the North, so again he strode away. He wished nothing more than to display to his compatriots that their faith in him was well-founded, that he indeed possessed courage and determination. He had not gone twenty paces, however, when again he realized that he was not being followed, and so again he turned back to find his fellows engaged in a heated argument.

"In making such a decision," declared Morton somewhat haughtily, "I cite the wisdom of my age and the virtue of my foresight." Freya rolled her eyes almost right up into her head and the falcon continued.

"Erik Blood-Axe stated that he was going to head toward the North today, and meet his brother in battle. Trust me, young Freya," he added, rather carefully, "we will find the king for whom we search if we make our way toward the North."

"And I say if we make our way toward the North, then we'll fall off the edge of the earth!" cried Freya. "I think maybe you don't want to find your wings at all! I think that you want to run away! I think that you want to spend the rest of your days skimpering over the snow like a bony, feathered rodent!"

Morton sighed. "Trust me, Freya the Falcon-Catcher. It is made very clear by these tracks in the snow: We will find the king we seek if we head toward the North."

Now we will leave Freya and Rolf and Morton the falcon, still in the middle of their argument, and travel not too far away from the small clearing in which they stand. In due time, I imagine they will come to some kind of agreement and set off on their journey, though it seems unnecessary to have to endure the entire debate.

16

Haakon the Good

LATER ON THIS SAME DAY, sometime in the middle of the afternoon, in a field at the northern edge of the same forest, a crowd has gathered to watch a man, not too young and not too old, gliding gracefully over the snow. Strapped onto his feet is a pair of flat sticks, and in his hands he carries a second pair of sticks, much narrower, which he uses to poke into the snow and propel himself forward.

As it happens, the people who have gathered have all got sticks strapped to their feet as well, and the man, not too old nor too young, is teaching them how to ski. In the minds of those gathered, this skiing lesson is merely a prelude to the real reason they have all come here on this afternoon, which is that they are much concerned about their leadership and their livelihood.

They are anxious and hopeful that their children will have good lives, and the sullen and brutal reign of Erik Blood-Axe has given them pause. So they have come to this field to hear the man that they have named their new king speak about the changes he wishes to make in their little part of the world. As such, they are just like people of any time who are concerned about their livelihoods. They're just like people in your world today, and that, I suppose, must be why I speak of them as though they are in the present. They are the Tronds of Trondheim, and they have gathered for the purpose of hearing Haakon the Good, the man they have chosen to lead them, make a speech.

"Now it's true," he continues, "that the Tronds of Trondheim no longer wish to be a part of this country. There is good reason for this, and that reason bears the name of Erik Blood-Axe, my own brother. My father united this country so that it would ultimately find peace within its borders, but Erik is always and forever going out and smiting people and making war here and there and everywhere, and never allowing his country-men to be at peace. I know men and women who would row beyond the endless ocean in order to get away from Erik and his ways. They would brave the unknown for the chance to forge a just society, yet Erik would call them cowards! But I say that Erik Blood-Axe is himself a coward! Too much of a coward to put down his sword and take on the true, hard role of kingship! And I say that if the Tronds of Trondheim have the will and the

courage to form a just and peaceful society right underneath his nose, then he will not have the nerve to stop
them. His warring and pillaging and slaughtering have
made him tired, and I say he will stay in the south of
this country and leave our people alone!"

Now the assembled Tronds are cheering. This is why
they've come: to listen to such comforting words as
these. As Haakon continues with his speech, it begins
to seem to all those assembled almost as if he is singing,
so welcome are his words to their ears.

"Tell me, what do you think?" he shouts. "Do you
think it's a good idea whereby you're able to inform a
great and lofty judge when he is wrong? Wouldn't that
be something?"

The cheer of the crowd goes up, telling Haakon
that indeed they do believe this would be something.
He goes on.

"And don't you think we should keep a fire on
every hill, that burns at night and tells the world our
Shire of Trondheim is secure and safe? Wouldn't that
be something?"

Yes, it would, the people cry, and stamp so hard
with their skis that many of them slip and fall over.
Skis are very tricky things, particularly when they've
only just recently been invented. Haakon continues:

"And, oh yes, one more thing: if we're going to
speak of civilizing . . ." Haakon hesitates a little, even
though the crowd is hanging on his every word. "I
wonder if you would all consent to become Christian?"

Oops. I forgot to mention. Athelston, King of England, Haakon's foster father, raised his adopted son as a Christian. The crowds of Tronds assembled here in Trondheim have not been equipped with this information, and so his request has come as an enormous shock: Christianity is a new religion from the south, and has spread through Europe like a forest on fire. It started in the Middle Eastern desert, where the sun is very hot, and, er ... I'm sure you can look it up. Perhaps it is too much for me to think I can tell you all about Christianity in the middle of my introduction to Haakon the Good. Suffice to say, er, it's a religion, and a big one at that. But in Trondheim, as in the whole of Norway, the people are Vikings. That is their way. That is their religion. Whether a warrior or not a warrior, a Viking is still a Viking, and a Christian is something else altogether.

A murmur of dissent runs through the crowd. These people are taken aback. All across Europe, whenever a king has decided to become a Christian, he decides on behalf of his people as well, and his people have had no choice but to convert. Only once in the whole long and bloody history of Europe has a Christian king merely, politely, asked his people to become Christian, and that is today, right here, in this field, in the year 933, in the middle of the afternoon, when Haakon the so-called Good, Haakon the Christian, stands on his skis before the Tronds of Trondheim.

"Well?" he says. "What do you say?"

There is a rumble of voices. Finally, a stout peasant named Grumhold steps forward. He is somewhat large and has a big belly, and it's not so much that he's brave exactly, although he is, but he mostly just thinks that anybody will heed the voice of reason if it is spoken clearly and briefly, and that nobody will ever fault the speaker for it. This isn't true, necessarily, as anyone who's spent a morning with Erik Blood-Axe will attest, but it is perhaps a good quality to have this belief, and, quite honestly, I have no idea why I'm devoting so much time and energy to telling you about this Grumhold fellow. He's never appeared before in this story, as you know, and he won't appear again. This is the last that we'll hear of him. It's just that the Tronds of Trondheim, all three hundred of those assembled, are individuals, each with their own particular heart and ideas and aspirations, and if I could tell you about each one of them, I would, since without them there would be no story, since without them there would be no king over them.

The point is mostly that our friend Grumhold will have to represent the individual voices of the Tronds of Trondheim, and he speaks the following:

"Sire," he says, in a low rumble that does not altogether mask his trepidation, "we wished to name you our king because we have heard that you are just and good. But, sire, your southern Christian God would not allow us to believe in Odin, god of all the North, nor would he allow us to believe in the rest of the northern gods, or heroes and giants and Valkyries of old, which are all told of in the Book of Edda. It has been many years since any of us has seen any of these creatures wandering through the forests of our land, but we still very much believe in them. If we made a choice such as this they would surely turn their backs on us and stay away from here forever. If you try to make us do this, we will have no choice but to overthrow you."

With that the man Grumhold steps back into the crowd. Everyone is silent and looking at the king, waiting to see how he might respond to their spokesman, who has somehow summoned the thoughts of the entire crowd forth from his mouth.

"Well!" says Haakon, after a further pause. "This fellow spoke well, didn't he?"

There was a murmur of assent from the nervous crowd.

"And it is my wish to agree with him," declares Haakon. "He respects the faith of his fathers, and so do you all. There is justice in that. Let some other king force you in years to come, not me."

There is yet another pause as the king's words sink in—a moment of suspended silence before, suddenly, the crowd cheers such as they have never cheered before. They cheer with relief and joy and the good fortune that they have found themselves a good and wise king.

And that, incidentally, is why Haakon the King was called Haakon the Good. Not because he was Christian, but because he did not force anybody to do something they didn't want to do. He let them believe what they wanted, despite the fact that he did not agree with it. He knew that he could lead them just as well despite the fact that he didn't share their beliefs. There are some people — Erik Blood-Axe, for instance — who might consider this to be a sign of Haakon's weakness, a sign that he is not, in fact, fit to be a king. Be that as it may, the Tronds of Trondheim are very happy on this snow-covered and gloomy grey day.

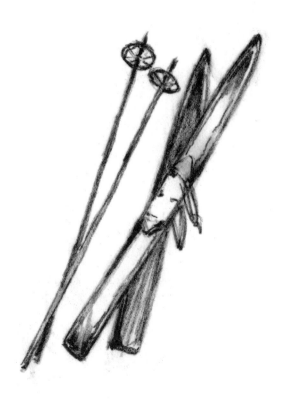

Freya and the King

A T THE EDGE of the field, between the field and the forest, stood Freya and Rolf and Morton. Well out in front of them, at the far end of the field, stood more people than Freya had ever seen gathered in one place in her life before. That must be an army, thought Freya to herself. And that must be their king.

"Well?" she said finally to Morton. "Look at that man. Is he not a king surrounded by his army?"

"I'd say so," said Morton, after a pause.

Freya looked at him. "And so is he the king we're looking for?"

"How many kings do you expect to reside in the general area?" asked Morton. "Do you still not believe I pointed you in the right direction?"

"I . . . I just wanted to make sure," said Freya. "Yes, you were right to make us go north instead of south. I . . . I apologize for doubting you."

"Oh no, that's entirely unnecessary." Morton would have been blushing if he were human. "My eyes. It's just that my eyes are not what they used to be." He was lying of course, but he continued. "I can only assume, by the size of the crowd, that this is the king we are looking for. You must step forward and address him."

"King?" asked Rolf.

"Yes," said Freya, and Morton nodded too, since if truth be told he actually understood much of their human tongue, though he could not utter a word of it. The three conferred quietly for a few minutes, drawing up a plan of approach. Finally, Morton and Rolf withdrew into the shadow of the trees, and Freya stepped boldly out into the open, striding as best she could through the snow toward the gathering.

"Well, now," said the king, "That is the smallest traveller I have ever laid eyes upon." All around him the people laughed.

"Hail, king!" cried Freya from across the field, seeing him look her way. And then she experienced the sensation of suddenly being regarded by more sets of eyes than she had ever seen. Her knees wobbled despite herself, and she wondered how she would be treated by this decidedly cruel King Erik. Still, she also noticed that there were women and children in this gathering, not just men. And if this was an army, where were their horses? For the first time, too, she noticed that everyone in the crowd had the oddest appendages strapped onto their feet.

"Hail, stranger!" called the king. This was good of him, since he could have cried "Hail, child!" or "Hail, little girl!" or something equally unbecoming. "How is it," he went on, "that you know I am a king?"

"You are clearly a king," called Freya, trying her best to emanate authority. "I can tell by the way you stand in the centre of all your people."

"You've seen many kings in your travels, then?" asked the king.

"No. In fact, you are the first king I have ever seen in my life."

"Well then, how do you know I'm not a physician, telling all these kind folk how to rid themselves and their livestock of worms?"

Freya was stumped by this. Of course, she knew for sure he was a king only because Morton had told her as much. Why would he try to hide the fact? Unless he was simply playing a game with her.

"As I came from the forest I heard a single word carried by the wind across the field to my ears," she ventured. "I thought maybe that word might have been spoken by you. I thought for a moment that I heard you speak the word 'justice.'"

"Well then," the man now turned to include his people. "if I speak of justice then it is even less likely I am a king."

"You mean to say that kings are unjust?" called Freya, swallowing the great feeling of trepidation that was overtaking her. "Well, I say you are a king and unjust!"

These were far and away the boldest words Freya had ever spoken in her whole life. Her head was spinning as she stepped closer toward the gathering, and she thought perhaps she was going to faint. She hoped that the distance between them was enough for her condition to escape his notice. The king, for his part, was smiling.

"And why do you say that?" he asked, with a merry and surprising sincerity.

"I am Freya the Cold," she announced, by way of explanation for her sudden fearful bout of shivers. "And Freya the Bold, the Falcon-Catcher. I demand, King Erik Blood-Axe, that you return to me some feathers that you have in your possession, so that I may in turn restore the dignity and power of a noble peregrine falcon. If you do not do what I ask then I can only say that you are hardly fit to be king, since there is no justice in a kingdom where the king would pull the wings from a bird!"

"Well, I agree with you," said the king, turning again to smile at his people, "but —"

"This is not a matter for smiling!" cried Freya the Small. "Return them to me! Else I will smite you with my giant!"

Much to Freya's dismay, the king's wide smile now broadened still further and then opened into a hearty laugh. He turned again and nodded approvingly to his people, many of whom were smiling and nodding and laughing as well. All of this was entirely bewildering to Freya, who had by this point utterly misplaced her fear. But then, almost as suddenly as it started, the ripple of laughter came to a halt and silence fell over the crowd. Freya turned to see that Rolf had chosen just this moment to step forth from the trees. He strode manfully into place directly behind her. To her great satisfaction she saw that he had uprooted a sizable tree and was holding it over his shoulder like a club.

"Well now," said the king, "I agree with you: he is a giant. I can't say I have ever seen his equal. However, I'm afraid I cannot give you what you ask, no matter how impressive your giant might be. And," he added, "no matter how much I would like to help you."

The king had spoken these with such seemingly genuine disappointment that Freya was left utterly, utterly confused. She felt like she had been the butt of some enormously complicated joke and did not yet understand what it was all about. Still, she held her ground.

"Why?" she asked. "Tell me why you cannot help us."

"For the simple reason, Freya the Bold, that you have mistaken me for my brother Erik, King of Norway."

There was no laughter at all at this revelation, since everyone who was gathered there that day could feel the brave young girl's embarrassment and dismay. She had spoken well and boldly to the cruel king of Norway without knowing that he had not even been present to hear her words, and they all knew it and were duly impressed. Freya, for her part, stood with her mouth open and blinked back the tears that were welling up. Really, she had been the victim of some kind of terrible bit of trickery. What's more, the perpetrator of this disgrace could have been none other than her supposed friend, the bird for whom she had been prepared to risk her life and limb, the allegedly noble Morton, unfeathered falcon.

"I . . . ," said Freya, who felt the eyes of all upon her once again. "I . . . ," and then she glanced back into the trees, from whence came no sign of Morton. Rolf still stood behind her though, proud to back up his big sister, proud to have brought the laughter of so many people to a halt.

"Not king?" he said to Freya.

"Wrong king," returned the dejected girl.

"Yes," said the king. "That is what you have done. My name is Haakon, Athelston's foster son. I have rule only over this humble shire you have stumbled into, and where you are welcome to stay. I venture to say that you are more fortunate than you know for having made this error, since the tyranny of my brother is such that he would only have plucked the wings from these noble words you have spoken here today. Such words would have meant nothing to him. I, on the other hand, have been presented with the vision of the bravest and noblest young girl I have ever had the honour to meet. Though we are not a wealthy people, I will spare no expense to make you feel welcome in these parts."

By this point, Freya quite wished to forget about her desire to retrieve the feathers, since these same feathers were only being sought to heal the wounds of a false and treacherous ingrate of a bird.

The king spoke again. "I must add, too, that if you consider yourself in any way to be in danger by King Erik, there is nothing to fear from him here. For like many a king with a cruel heart, my brother is really a coward, and I dare say he would never venture into my claim."

"Ak! Ak! Ak!" A call came suddenly from the trees, followed in a moment by Morton himself, who skittered awkwardly across the field and came to light right next to Freya. Freya curled up her little fingers and was all set to punch him right on the curve of his beak when the king spoke up again.

"Well now," said Haakon, "this must be your falcon."

Freya glanced coldly at Morton, who spoke quietly to her.

"Forgive me, young Freya the Bold, but it seemed to me that Haakon the Good would be more willing to help us with our cause if he saw for himself how bravely you would present yourself before his brother. Notice how you have gained his undivided attention."

"Well, you could have told me," countered Freya, huffily.

"If I had told you, it would not have been the same. In order to speak boldly, it seems to me you have to have some little taste of fear in your heart. Without fear it is not possible to be brave. This good king would not have given you cause to fear him, and so you would not have spoken so well."

"Still, it was a nasty trick."

"Forgive me, Freya, but now I have urgent and important words to speak, and you must translate them for me."

Freya sighed. She felt again the same wave of irritation she'd experienced at having to translate for her brother. It seemed there was nothing more trying to her patience than this. Still, there was nothing to be done. Morton had turned to face the king, who was filled with shock and pity at the bony and dishevelled state of this bird. The falcon stretched himself as tall as he could, ruffled and smoothed his few feathers and called in a loud voice.

"Ak! Ak ak ak ak ak ak ak!"

Morton's words held such gravity that Freya immediately forgot her anger. She turned and looked at Morton and her face went pale. And then she turned back again, feeling the sudden weight of a great and new responsibility, and spoke in clear Norwegian to the King. "My friend the falcon says to tell you that you are wrong in saying King Erik will never cross into your claim. He says to tell you that in fact King Erik will cross into your claim tonight."

"Really!" called the King, somewhat bemused.

"Ak ak ak ak ak ak!" called Morton. "Ak ak ak ak!"

"He says to tell you . . . ," Freya gulped. "that King Erik says he will burn down your shire and melt all the snow in your skiing grounds," she called.

"Tell him," said Morton, turning to Freya. "Tell him that Erik has opened an old Viking cask of hatred, such that Norway has not sipped in many a year."

Freya turned to call again to the king. "He says to tell you that Erik has opened up a cask of beer," she said, and then realized she had got it wrong.

"I beg your pardon?" asked the puzzled king, as laughter rippled again through the crowd and Freya's face grew red with fresh embarrassment. She turned and glared hotly at Morton, but he had not realized anything had gone amiss, and spoke up again.

"Ak a—"

"Shut up!" she shouted. "I'm not finished yet!"

"It sounded fine to me," said Morton.

"It wasn't fine, it was ridiculous," said Freya. "It sounded like Erik was inviting his brother to drink some beer! You know, it's not going to be easy to translate for you if you're going to speak in the elevated tones of poetry."

"Oh," said the falcon. "Yes, I see. We warrior birds can get a bit too grand sometimes. I'll try to be simpler, for what it's worth."

"I would appreciate that."

Freya turned back to face the king and composed herself again to speak. "What I meant was," she said, "he said to tell you that Erik is angry."

"I see," said the king, and Freya sighed with relief that they were back on the course. She turned and nodded for Morton to continue.

"Ak!" said Morton, trying to keep it all as simple as possible. "Ak ak!"

Freya called again to the King. "My friend says to tell you that he was sent here with the news that you are to meet King Erik in battle on the Fields of Snorre this very night!"

She turned back and looked at Morton, who nodded to her that he was finished.

"Is that all your friend has to say?" asked the ling. Freya nodded. "And is that really what he says?" Again Freya nodded and the king went on. "Well, I must confess that I have some difficulty believing you. Do you truly profess to speak the language of birds?"

"I do not profess it," said Freya, trying not to sound annoyed and disrespectful. "It's just the truth."

"Well," said King Haakon, "I confess that we all have been more than aptly entertained by your carnival show. I see now, however, that though you speak boldly, you are but a child, and have a child's imagination."

These words came as a crushing blow to the three standing together between the field's edge and the king. Freya looked at the people gathered and saw that the smiles had not left their faces, that these same smiles, in fact, seemed permanently fixed. She was so annoyed by all their revelry that she thought she might scream. Turning away from all their stupid, beaming faces she caught a sad, dull golden eye of Morton. It winked at her, catching her off guard.

"So, my Freya the Bold," he said, "I thought this might have been the king to seek. I thought he might have provided us with some well-needed company when it came time for us to face our great adversary. But it seems you were correct in your desire to go south, my girl. There's nothing for us here in the North. It seems we shall face our tyrant king alone."

"What shall we do?" asked Freya.

"What else can we do? You said the three of us would be enough," said Morton. "I should have believed you."

"Shall we go, then?" asked Freya.

"We shall." said Morton.

Freya looked up and nodded for Rolf to drop his tree and come. The three then turned to walk back into the southern woods.

"Wait a moment!" shouted the king. "I did not say that you had to leave, only that you had an interesting imagination. It is my wish for you to return with us to our village, where we will have a great feast in honour of you and your friends."

Freya turned. "It is my wish, however, to take my leave. I have an urgent appointment to keep with the king of Norway."

18

Backed Up by the Beaky

AS FREYA, Rolf, and Morton turned again to go, they were greeted by the strangest thing that any of them had ever seen. A man had just hopped out of the bushes and was skittering toward them, his arms aloft and akimbo. From the sound that rose from the crowd it was apparent that the Tronds had seen him too. He ground to a halt in the snow just as Freya realized with tremendous shock that he was the man from before, the servant who had ambushed them from the bushes. Now, however, he was much transformed. His clothes were tattered and torn and on his face he bore a curiously kind expression, clear to her even at this distance. Strangest of all, he stood now in an odd position, craning his long neck so that his head dangled over his right shoulder, and holding his left foot off the ground, all the while emitting strange muttering sounds.

"Ak!" he cried. Yes, distinctly. Freya heard it. So did Rolf and Morton and Haakon the Good and all the assembled Tronds. "Ak," was most definitely what he said, though Freya remarked to herself that the sound didn't seem to mean anything. Then he spoke again, directly to the king.

"I bring news from Erik Blood-Axe, the box-headed Axe-nose. Your big brother, who refers to you, by the way, as his baby brother, wants to meet you in battle. He's brought his armour and his weapons and his Vikings all this way, and he—" here the man turned and gestured toward the South, "he will be waiting tonight over there, in the Field of Snorre, just beyond the forest."

"And who," asked Haakon, puzzled, "are you?"

"I," answered the messenger, with the first surge of pride he had ever felt, "am The Beaky. Formerly of the Bikki. Formerly Bikki Number Four, but then transformed through the great wisdom of King Erik to Bikki Number O, and from there found my own way to my own Beaky, the One and Only, which same name suits me just fine."

Bikki to Beaky. It sounded to all assembled as if this strange character had barely changed his name at all and was merely babbling. The king spoke to him again. "And you bring this news officially from King Erik?"

The featherless Beaky reached into his pocket, cackled and produced the king's seal he'd always carried by virtue of being a Bikki.

"Here," he said, spinning the little piece of gold quite accurately through the air and into Haakon's open hand. "It's a pretty thing but I don't need it anymore. You can have it."

Then he turned to address the party of three who stood and regarded him. "My apologies to you all for my odious and decidedly unsympathetic behaviour of yesterday. I can't say it was entirely out of character, but I assure you I've had somewhat of a change of heart."

"I'd say so," said Freya, who couldn't really help herself.

"Indeed, indeed, it's true, I have. The Beaky's my name, as you may have heard, and I am at your service."

Here he made a deep and humble bow, and Freya was struck with a funny observation: she had been trying to figure out who this strange man had been reminding her of, and it suddenly occurred to her that it was Morton. It was as if this man were playing the part of her falcon friend in some kind of performance. He had wrapped his head in a black scarf to create a kind of cowl and he'd rolled up his pants to expose white stockings on long, skinny legs. There was more to observe than this, much more, but the king had completed his examination of the gold seal and now spoke gravely to the whole assembly.

"Well," he said, "this seal is certainly official, though it would seem to have been brought to me by the most unconventional means. So it's true: my brother, Erik

Blood-Axe, wishes to meet me in battle. Well, I declare to you today, Tronds of Trondheim, that I simply cannot agree to this declaration of war!"

"What?" said Morton, who could not believe his ears.

"Under no circumstances will I meet my brother in battle tonight or any night! He thinks of nothing but pillage and slaughter: It's a terrible thing to witness!"

"But that's the whole point!" cried Morton. "If you are to prevent him from having his pillage and slaughter then you must meet him on the battlefield! That's the whole point!"

His squawkings and twitterings were left untranslated, however, though they did draw the attention of the curious Beaky, who scampered over for a closer look at his former quarry. King Haakon went on with his speech.

"I'm tired of hearing about King Erik and his battles," he said. "I'm tired of hearing about Erik and his campaigns and his unpleasant ways. Let him fight a battle by himself. He can stand in the centre of the Field of Snorre and swing his sword all the way around so that it strikes him in the back of the head! That's what I think of Erik and his battles!"

"But he'll burn down your shire!" protested the untranslated Morton.

"You know," continued Haakon, "I was told a story once by a fellow who had witnessed first-hand these warrior ways. He told me that my brother once surrounded and attacked an iceberg. Imagine! An iceberg! He did it for the simple reason that he thought it was a garrisoned stash of silver. He had never seen an iceberg before and assumed that it contained riches simply because it was big and glinted in the sun! He attacked this iceberg and lost thirty-seven men. Thirty-seven men! My brother is greedy and stupid. I won't fight him."

Morton was shaking his head. "I am a bird of prey," he muttered, "a creature of war. I don't understand how a king can speak of not fighting when another king has declared war on him. I don't understand it at all."

But Freya was giving her full attention to the king, who now spoke again to her. "I'll tell you what I will do, however, young Freya the Falcon-Talker. I will come along with you to these Fields of Snorre, and I will tell my brother to return his stolen feathers to your friend. That is something I will do."

"Thank you very much," called Freya, as Morton muttered behind her, "Well, how is he going to do that? Without meeting Erik in battle, how is he going to demand anything at all from him? This man is a fool!"

"He spoke of justice," whispered Freya quickly. "And he's a king. I don't know why you must be so impolite."

"And I don't know how he can get justice if he's weak," muttered Morton. "His English education has destroyed his Viking ways! This king is a coward."

"If this king is a coward, then why is he coming to meet his brother at all?"

"Because he's also a fool. Maybe he's more of a fool than he is a coward."

"Don't be so rude," said Freya. "There are many ways of doing things."

"Not where Erik Blood-Axe is concerned. Where Erik is concerned, there is only one way, and that way is war."

As Freya and Morton argued between themselves, and Rolf waited patiently for their twittering to stop, the king was speaking to his people.

"Well!" he cried. "What do you think? Shall we all ski together across the border into Erik's land? He will not seek to fight us when he sees how we stand as one!"

A cheer went up from the crowd. Morton continued to mutter to himself about how they were all a bunch of drunken and suicidal fools.

"You see?" said Haakon, turning back to Freya. "There is much we can accomplish if we all stand together. Young girl, you can be certain that we'll get your feathers. We'll shame my brother, call him a bully of birds and children, until he has no choice but to hand them over. And if he brandishes his glinty weapons, we'll laugh!"

Freya though to herself that she had never heard tell of a merrier king than this one. "We accept your offer," she declared in her most official-sounding voice, as Morton's eyes beside her rolled and faded into a duller shade of gold.

"Night is beginning to fall!" called the king to his

people. "We must set off! What a pleasant opportunity this is for us to practise our skiing!" This last line, fully understood by Morton except for the one word "skiing," was almost too much for him to bear, but he remained silent.

And so they set off, the Tronds of Trondheim, Haakon the Good, Freya, Rolf, Morton, and the featherless Beaky taking up the rear, flapping his arms, squawking and hopping his way, proudly, defiantly, and without complaint, through this now three-times-covered terrain.

Three hundred skiers make their way through a grey dusk toward the South, led by a merry Christian king. Morton sits perched upon the shoulder of the giant Rolf, and Freya runs beside them, doing her best to keep up. The tattered old falcon is wrapped in a cowl of silence, turning his head in small movements. If he could speak to you, reader, listener, in this moment, if he knew that you were there with him, this is what he would say:

Hearken, you who speak the English tongue
How we proceed:
Naive brave girl,
Tall small boy,
A falcon without feathers—that is me.
We march to a battle that we cannot call a battle,

For if we call it a battle
In the midst of the battle,
Then the man we call king won't fight!
This man we call king will not fight!

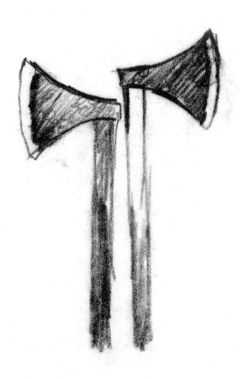

The Feathered Cloak

HERE WE ARE in history, the history of the Viking Wars, the true history of Norway. You may ask how, if this represents the true history of Norway, can there be at the very centre of our tale the character of a falcon who can speak to a little girl? All I can say, in my defence, is that most of the men and women who wish to be taken seriously in their study of history will only relate the stories they consider to be true. Oftentimes, they have to defend their stories to roomfuls of scholars. They get a little nervous. They leave out the tales that got told and retold by parents to their children, passed on over hundreds of years until no one is certain anymore where they came from. When they come across evidence of giants and Valkyries and talking birds, they simply disregard it and record a version of the events that seems more reasonable and suitable to their task. History therefore records that Erik Blood-Axe, King of Norway, met his brother Haakon the Good on the Fields of Snorre sometime in the year 933, or, some say, 934, and that Haakon the Good somehow emerged as the victor even though he was not inclined to raise his arms in battle. Thus succession is achieved, the tale is told, and history marches forward into the future. The author of this tale, however, can hardly be considered a serious historian, and so has nothing to lose by telling you how it all really happened on that day in Norway on the Fields of Snorre in the year 933. I have no need of history books, since, as I've said before, I was there.

King Erik Blood-Axe stood below his feathered banner, surrounded by his Bikki and backed by his Viking army, looking every inch a victor in advance of the battle. Emerging from the forest in front of him was perhaps the most unwarlike assemblage of people he'd ever seen: an army of skiers, led by a skiing king who could only be his brother, Haakon the Good, said by some to be a Christian. This brother, whom he had never actually seen before, struck him as a slight figure, small and soft, with a boyish demeanour of unweathered features. That such a man would presume to be a king stuck in his craw somewhat. Erik considered how under different circumstances he might have felt affection for this brother, perhaps even have deigned to protect him from the world, allowed him to study the disciplines of music or poetry or portrait painting—some gift of art that would create a lasting legacy from the reign of Erik Blood-Axe. He didn't know where such non-Viking thoughts as these came from, and suspected that perhaps he had been settled too long. In any case, he wasn't about to encourage his brother in any artistic disciplines or protect him from the world, but rather was about to meet him in battle and slay him. Such an undertaking, he felt confident, would put an end to these lingering thoughts once and for all. He would strike at this feeble brother and watch with satisfaction as he slid away on sliding skis into the arms of Death.

Haakon the Good, his army behind him, came to a stop some distance away from the other army. He called cheerfully across the divide.

"Brother?"

"Yes," called Erik, with dark humour, "I am your brother, though from this day hence I plan to be an only child."

"I do not wish to disappoint you, brother," called Haakon, "but I have not come to make war on you. I rather come today to speak to you on behalf of a young girl who talks to birds."

Erik was dumbfounded by this and the thought suddenly occurred to him that the slight fellow who stood opposite him was perhaps insane. For a moment he didn't know what to say, and then Haakon continued.

"It would seem, Erik, that you have borrowed the feathers of an acquaintance of hers."

"Ah," said Erik finally, and looked up at the feathered banner that hung behind him from its high staff. Unexpected as this was, there was something about it that pleased him, since it surely meant that Haakon the Good had encountered his featherless falcon after all. The bungling Bikki Number Four had not entirely failed, then, in his mission.

"Well," he called at last. "What if I have?"

"It seems to me," called Haakon, "that these feathers in question are of far more use to this bird than they are to you. I think perhaps it's time that you gave them back."

Erik stood and regarded his brother for a few moments and then stepped back and roared with laughter. He laughed so hard in fact that he fell down in the snow, causing a ripple of tension to surge through the army of Vikings that stood behind him. Two hundred warriors all drew their swords as one, though they did not otherwise move, and Erik rolled in the snow and laughed and laughed until he stopped. Then he stood up again and spoke, and his voice was equal parts ice and mirth.

"So, brother," he said, "you have declared yourself king of the Tronds. Then you have ventured even deeper into the heart of my territory than you already were, just so you might request that I return the feathers to a bird."

"Yes," said Haakon, "except I did not declare myself king of the Tronds. This mantle of kingship was thrust upon me."

"Well, you're a good boy then, aren't you?" said Erik. "You're a good boy, always doing what you're told. But I tell you, brother, the way I see it, if you want something, you've got to take it yourself. That's the first brotherly lesson I give to you today. You want to take this feathered banner from me? There it is, brother." He pointed up at the lifeless mascot on its staff. "There it is. Come take it. Seize my feathers from me."

"I cannot agree with you," called Haakon. Behind him his army of Tronds grew restless. They had hid all their children behind them in the forest and were beginning to grow nervous at the thought that they would actually have to fight. Still, they were prepared.

"If I try and take these feathers," called Haakon, "you won't let me. You'll probably strike me with your sword and kill me. No, I think rather that you should give them to me."

"Ah," cried Erik, "that's a problem, isn't it? I think you should take my banner and you think I should give it you. Indeed, that is a problem, unless you consider that this feathered banner of mine is, in fact, a banner of war, and it would mean the same thing in the end whether I give it to you or whether you take it. It would mean that I have ceded victory to you in this field of battle. Therefore, brother, there is only one solution to this problem of ours."

Erik drew his sword and stepped forward. Behind him the army of Vikings stepped forward as one.

"Fight, Haakon!" cried Erik. "The fool thinks he'll live forever if only he does not fight. But old age won't spare you even if the spear does!"

"I agree with you," called Haakon, "but—"

"Then fight!" cried Erik.

As Erik said this, two very surprising things happened. First, Morton the falcon appeared, much to Erik's amazement. Second, the Tronds all suddenly started bustling about. They shifted on their feet, leaned forward, and unfastened their skis. Then each of the Tronds of Trondheim grasped his left ski and lifted it high over his head. For the Tronds of Trondheim were a very practically minded people, and, unbeknownst to Haakon, they had given very specific instructions to the smiths who had fashioned their skis. In creating each pair, the smiths had doubled the left one as a fully functioning broadsword, complete with hilt, guard, and razor-sharp blade coming to an impressive point. This innovation had the unfortunate effect of making them somewhat dangerous and unbalanced as skis, but as broadswords they were perfectly reliable.

So the Tronds were armed, and Morton the falcon was rushing headlong at the king of the opposing camp.

Morton had watched the events unfold from the shoulder of young Rolf, who stood somewhat nervously at the edge of the forest in the back of the Trondheim crowd. Behind him, all the Trondish children were peeking out from the trees. Beside and below him, on the ground, Freya stood on her toes and strained to get a better look. Morton knew it dismayed Freya to have been pressed to the back of the crowd, to have been considered a child even though it was mostly her business that had brought them all here.

Over the heads of the crowd, Morton watched his former king taunt the younger Haakon. It was clear to him that Haakon was no fighter. Morton wondered what to do. The events of the day had shifted from a simple quest to regain his wings—transformed, in fact, into a full-fledged potential for war. Looking down again he saw, beside Freya, the man who had been their former adversary, the odd fellow, The Beaky, who flitted about and seemed to behave like some kind of bird. Morton found this man's behaviour slightly distasteful, disrespectful even, but it was clear that he was no longer an enemy. On the contrary, this man seemed to have a need to watch over the children and keep them safe from harm. Considering this, Morton began to feel freer to forgo his own protective instincts and hurl himself into the fray. Ridiculous as this man might be, he was as knowledgeable of the ways of Erik Blood-Axe as was Morton himself, and could not be underestimated as an ally. In fact, it was very likely that the two most capable fighters in the entire army were himself and this mirror-image bird-man, this self-proclaimed Beaky the One and Only, former henchman to Erik. Morton opened his beak to speak.

"Ak!" he called, catching the attention of The Beaky.

Out in front, Erik had drawn his sword against Haakon.

The Beaky looked up and saw the flashing gold eyes of the falcon upon him.

"Ak," said Morton again: Protect these children.

"Are you talking to me, falcon?" asked The Beaky.

"Ak," said Morton again, to press home his point, and then took off.

Our wreckage of a falcon should here have crashed straight to the ground, but determination kept him aloft as he hopped from head to shoulder to head through the crowd. Scampering as best he could, trying not to hurt anyone with his talons, Morton made his way to the front. Hurtling over Haakon's shoulder, he landed heavily in the field between the two camps and saw the surprised face of his former king just before he dove into it. Erik, for his part, knew how to deal with such an errant bird of prey, though he was somewhat distracted by the sudden movement of the Trondish army and their sudden warrior-like transformation. Still, he dropped his sword and, even as Morton managed to slash his cheek, grasped the bird and threw it to the ground at his feet.

"Ah, my falcon," cried Erik, addressing everyone it seemed but Morton. "I wondered when he would appear.

He's been unhooded and his blood is up! That's more like my old bird! Still, he's not much of a flier anymore, is he?"

"Speak to my face, tyrant!" cried Morton, though Erik understood only the sound of a great unbroken shriek. As Morton leapt at him again, the king drew his short sword and slashed at the bird's claws even as they slashed at him. Again, Morton hit the dirt, bleeding from his foreleg.

"Stand!" bellowed Erik to his men, who were themselves straining at the bit to surge forward into the fight. "I see I have many former friends to greet this night. My falcon has remembered how to use his claws. If he were not such a wreck, if his feathers did not hang high above my army instead of on his back, he might serve as a worthy opponent! He might even serve me again as a hunting hawk!"

"Never!" shrieked Morton and leapt again at the king as the short sword flashed in the light that burned from his predatory eyes.

Freya, for her part, had run, suddenly leaving The Beaky far behind, and Rolf had bounded in front of her to blaze a trail through the army of the Tronds. No one could stop her with a giant to lead the way. As she ran, she heard the king address his former bird in a loud and mocking voice, and she heard Morton answer and wished that she could translate for him.

"Rolf!" she cried as they reached the front, "the wings!" She pointed and Rolf stopped to look, since he could still only do one thing at a time, and saw the staff from which hung Morton's feathers.

He saw that it was surrounded everywhere by Vikings bearing sharp swords and felt a moment of panic surge up inside himself. Then, as he stood, he struggled through his thoughts to say out loud the words that Morton had only yesterday spoken to him through his sister. In a voice that could be heard as far away as Iceland, Rolf shouted, "TIGHT SPOT, BUT ROLF CAN DO THIS BEST FOR HE IS WISE AND BIG!"

Fourteen words, if any that turned their heads had had time to count them. Then Rolf ran. For the first time in his life, he ran toward a thing rather than away from it, and in his running he felt a power surge up inside of him that was bigger than anything he had ever felt or known or seen. As he ran, the ground shook around him and he saw the Viking warriors fall back, their eyes round and full of fear. In a moment of blazing speed, he had crossed the divide that separated the armies and seized the staff in his fist. As a cry rose from the sturdy Vikings, Rolf turned and hurled the staff like a spear, feathered banner and all, directly at their king. In the same moment, the two armies rushed at one another. Several Vikings in fact were rushing now at him, and as the staff clattered to the ground at the fighting Erik's feet, the battle had begun.

Morton was lying in the snow. The battle raged all around him, Rolf striding above the throng. Nearby, the two kings were hacking at one another. In the moments that Morton had taken to distract the king, Haakon had discovered that he himself had a broadsword strapped to his left foot, removed his skis and was now as well-armed as the Tronds that surged forward all around him. It had surprised him that the Tronds had revealed themselves as a warlike people. He had no time to dwell on it, however, and was grateful to be armed and defending himself against the frightening and powerful blows of his brother.

Freya had seen her falcon receive a terrible blow from the cruel king, had seen him fall to the ground without rising. Now she was pushing her way through the press of warriors. Small child that she was, she was all but ignored by the fighters on both sides. Still it took some time, and before she got to the fallen falcon, she saw another reach him and kneel down by his side. It was The Beaky, and he held in his hands the feathered cloak from the fallen staff. Morton lay in the snow with his eyes closed and did not see.

"Morton!" she cried as she got to his side, and The Beaky thrust the feathers into her arms.

Morton opened his eyes and looked at her. Again, she saw the keen intelligence that shimmered behind them, but she still could not read his expression.

"Morton," she said again, stirring her gentleness with panic, "your wings."

Morton blinked slowly and spoke to the young girl. "Freya the Falcon-Catcher. So it is you that has stuck by me, brave girl. You have brought me back to my wings."

Freya looked up and caught the eye of The Beaky, who divined what had just been said and nodded in a small bird-like gesture. "I stood by as they were taken away from him," he said quietly.

"Freya the Bold," Morton spoke again, "I need to rest a moment. Take my feathers and sling them over your own shoulders. See how they fit."

Freya stood up in shock. All around her, swords and skis clashed and warriors grunted and shouted and fell. Erik seemed to be getting the better of Haakon, who still fought valiantly. No others came between these two brother kings as they fought. Rolf was striding about, picking up Viking warriors and hurling them at one another. He was bleeding from a couple of pricks in his leg, but didn't seem to mind.

Freya looked uncertainly back at Morton. She began to protest. "How can I—"

"Don them, stubborn girl!" shouted Morton. "Respect your elders! Do as I say!"

Freya hesitated for another moment and regarded the clutch of feathers in her hand. Hanging there, it seemed now like the kind of cloak her father would wear to protect himself from the cold. She looked one last time at the sharp golden eyes of her falcon.

"Don them," he whispered to her in a low throttle. Freya slipped the wings over her shoulders.

The inside of the cloak felt like honeycomb that seemed to seep through her clothes and adhere to her skin, giving her a sensation of warmth she hadn't felt since the days before the sun disappeared behind its heavy hood of clouds. She heard a high, piercing cry arise from somewhere nearby on the battlefield and in another moment she felt as though she had been taken swiftly onto Rolf's high shoulders, from there to a house-top, from there to a high hill, from there to a mountaintop, from there to a place above the clouds where the sky was a darkening blue and the setting sun shone brilliant and everywhere and she was flying.

It was true. The feathers held fast to her, fixed to some foreign bone and sinew sprung unbidden from her shoulders, and she was flying. Like a bird. Like Morton in former days. In a single shining moment, she had forgotten the battle that had raged somewhere and was now far away. Freya flew. She flew as though it was something she had done for her whole life. She soared and swooped and felt herself a newborn in the sun. A second piercing cry arose from somewhere nearby and Freya suddenly realized that it had come from her. In an instant, she was aware of herself again, though utterly transformed. She remembered the battle and the king and she remembered Morton on the field, the true possessor of these wings. She remembered how his golden eyes had closed again as she had donned these wings, and as the sun dipped now below the horizon she knew that she had to return.

All around The Beaky, everything was still. Warriors stood, their arms limp at their sides and looked up to where they'd seen a hole open in the clouds and the young winged girl fly through and disappear. He himself stood with his mouth open and his eyes on the sky. Morton lay at his feet and the smile on his face was so apparent that even Erik Blood-Axe would have seen it, at least if he were looking.

As it was, the eyes of Erik Blood-Axe were on the sky, as were the eyes of Haakon the Good, and Rolf the Ranger, and the three Bikki, and all the Vikings and all the Tronds with their broadsword skis. They had all heard the first cry. The Beaky had witnessed the cry first-hand, seen it come like a living thing from the mouth of the transformed Freya, seen it emerge like a bird and lead the young girl into a flaming burst of flight. He all but forgot his eccentric bird-ways in that moment and stood as a human like the rest. And then, a moment later he heard, along with all the rest, another cry and then another, and then from the forest there emerged two women astride great black horses in full gallop. The Beaky no longer feared the Valkyries, even as they rode straight down into the centre of the battlefield, and the warriors parted the way before them like so much long grass. They came to a halt before the two kings and regarded the sky like all the rest. In these moments that followed Freya's flight into the sky, the sun had set and the field was shrouded in darkness, but the armour and the eyes and the wings of these women shone with a fiery light that reflected off the gleaming black hides of their horses. In the darkness, no one saw the clouds part again, but another moment passed in which everyone remained standing and still, and another, and then Freya had alighted and was standing among them, next to The Beaky, beside her beloved falcon, before whom she now knelt down to attend.

"Well, Freya," said Morton quietly. "Look at that. They fit."

Freya nodded and picked up her falcon, who now seemed so much smaller than herself. She cradled him in her arms and her wings pulled in and folded around to cover them both.

"Morton," she spoke softly, rocking him. "My Morton. Morton, my Morton, Morton, my Morton."

"I think," he whispered, basking in the warmth of his own wings covering him, "that you had best attend to your people."

Freya looked up. For the first time, she saw the pair of women, standing close on their horses and silently regarding her. One stood closer to her than the other, and Freya noticed that she was not fair like so many people of the North, but rather raven-haired, like Freya herself, though her hair, she could see, even in this darkness, was streaked with silver. Freya looked around herself and saw the standing armies, saw The Beaky, saw her brother Rolf who had approached and was standing close to her, looking from Freya to the women, from Freya to the women and back again, tears standing in his eyes, his mouth forming a single, whispered word. "Wings," said Rolf to Freya. "Wings, wings, wings."

Freya smiled and nodded to her brother. "Morton's wings," she said. "Morton's beautiful feathered cloak, rescued by my brave and giant brother."

Then Erik Blood-Axe spoke up. "Well!" he shouted, his voice puffed up with the pride of kingship. "Look at this. Full-bloom Valkyries, Choosers of the Slain, come to honour us in our battle! And here!" Now he turned to his army and pointed to Rolf. "Here is a giant such as we have never seen outside the size-making words of the Edda! All of you!" Now he addressed Freya and Rolf and the women. "You're Vikings!"

Freya looked up at the women on their horses, the raven-haired one still regarding her with a warmth that she could not name. They had seemed not to heed the words of the king of Norway, so Freya now turned to him herself, and spoke.

"Yes," she said.

"Yes!" shouted Erik. "Yes! You're Vikings! As I am a Viking! King again this night of a united Norway like my father before me! Surely that is why you have come, you Valkyries and your giant. You have come to honour me in my victory!"

"We are Vikings," said Freya, and in her arms Morton nodded.

"And this is the time of the Vikings!" shouted the proud Erik. "We polish our swords so bright that they light the paths we take at night! We drink our ale and plunge into battle, warriors all!"

All around him the Vikings and the Tronds stood silent. No one was fighting. No army had emerged so far as the victor in this halted fray. Freya stood, still holding the tender falcon in her fast-strengthening arms.

"You, girl—you shall be my general. And this giant at your side, he will be my general, too. With warriors such as the two of you, I have no more need for the Bikki! In the coming Viking conquest of the world, you two shall be second only to your commander and your king!"

Standing nearby, The Beaky could not help but feel a twinge of sympathy for his former fellows. He stole a glance their way. All three were nearby, looking hard at the ground, daring not to even look at one another in this moment of keen betrayal from their king. It had been mere hours since The Beaky had himself felt such shame, though he had by now travelled a lifetime away from it; still, he blushed in spite of himself. Freya looked over at him, the only Bikki she knew. He smiled warmly at her, and Freya turned again to the king.

"No," she said.

Erik blinked. "No?" he said.

Freya turned now and looked at King Haakon, though she spoke to Erik Blood-Axe. "No," she said.

Erik turned and followed her eyes to the brother who stood beside him. "You would follow him?" he said. "Haakon? Haakon the Good? He's not even a fighter." Now he turned to include the Valkyries on their horse.

"I've even heard that he is a Christian! So you would all rather become Christians, would you? Rather than follow a Viking into glory?"

Now it was Haakon's turn to speak. "I asked my people already if they would become Christians. They said no."

Erik blanched. "You asked them?" he said, unable to believe his ears.

"Yes," said Haakon. "And they said no."

"What kind of a king are you, anyway?" Here Erik turned back to Freya and Rolf. "Not only is he a Christian, but he's a coward king, who would allow his people to do whatever they want!"

"This king may not be a warrior like the bold King Erik Blood-Axe," said Freya. "But I heard him speak today of justice and how to find it. When he spoke, his words came out like music."

"That's probably because he sang them!" shouted Erik.

"His words to me were welcome," said Freya, allowing a bit of ice into her voice as she cradled the still Morton. "For there can be no justice in a kingdom in which the king would tear the wings from a bird. This king," she turned again to Haakon, "spoke of justice. And if I am born to be a warrior, then I will be the warrior that stands behind his weakness and calls it king."

All around the Tronds and even the Vikings pressed forward to hear such eloquent words pass through the lips of the young girl who had changed before their eyes into a Valkyrie.

"No, but you don't understand this kind of king," said Erik. He was almost pleading now, as the Tronds and the Vikings came closer. "This kind of king will say anything! That's how the weak of heart come to power. They never speak a single word of simple truth!"

Erik stepped back and looked at the two armies. The spirit had all but gone out of him, and not only did the Tronds observe this, but the Vikings saw it too. "So this is Ragnarök," he said to all of them standing there. "This is the end of the Viking world, when the Valkyries and the giants turn their backs on Viking warriors and follow a Christian into the future—a future in which they themselves will disappear, along with Odin, the gods, and all the ancient tales of glory!"

He took another step back and looked into the faces of his Norsemen. He was almost weeping now, but his blood was seething within him. "I want no part of it!" he shouted. "I'm a wanderer! A warrior born. A Viking!"

Erik glared at Rolf and Freya, and even the women on their horses, who had not once cast their eyes upon him. "I hate this settled life anyway!" he shouted. "It's shameful what we have done today: come to a battle the likes of which the world has never seen! Because it was not a battle at all! I'm going to sail to England, and when I get there I will raise such an army as the Viking age has never seen! And then, one day, I shall return with my army and break this country into little pieces!

Only in a land of turmoil can the qualities of the Viking heart be truly forged."

Erik strode now toward his horse. "I trade my kingly life for that!" he shouted behind him as he mounted. Then he turned his horse to face the armies and spoke one last time.

"Anyone who wishes to stay in a Norway united under a Christian king may stay. Anyone who wishes to follow a Viking into the future, come with me now!"

And then he turned and rode away. In a moment, the three Bikki were on their horses and riding behind him, to the South. Some Vikings trudged away in their armour to follow them, but not many. Most had no desire to leave their homes in the North, in their glorious wintered Norway. Erik continued to ride without looking back until he disappeared over a far hill, barely seen in the darkness. The Beaky watched him go, feeling again the burr of banished loyalty pierce his heart. He spoke quietly then in the voice of history:

> Haakon, Athelston's adopted son,
> Was given all of Norway,
> While his brother,
> Erik Blood-Axe,
> Mounted his horse and rode away.

There was a moment of silence as everyone stood. Then the two winged women turned suddenly away and spurred their horses toward the North.

"Wait!" cried Freya, her wings fluttering around her head and the cradled Morton. The women stopped and turned and regarded her silently.

"Who are you?" Freya spoke to the woman with raven hair and streaks of grey. In her voice was the sound of a child's longing. The woman gently spurred her horse forward and rode slowly up until she was sitting just above Freya. She reached down and touched the girl's face and looked into her eyes. Black eyes into black eyes. Smiling for an instant and forever.

"Thank you," said Freya.

The woman sat up again, tall on her horse. Then she turned and in a moment was beside her partner. The two let out one last high piercing cry of farewell and set off at a gallop. A moment later they were gone, disappeared into the woods.

Freya stood, the quiet Morton still cradled in her arms, and watched the women ride away. Then she looked upon the figure she held. The cowl of black that covered his head had specks of grey, newly tinted it seemed through this evening's events. She spoke softly to him, quietly cooing. It was clear he was injured. He opened his dull gold eyes again and looked up at her. As he spoke, her wings fluttered, responding to the soft buzz of his voice travelling from his body into hers.

"Did you see the sun?" he whispered. Freya nodded.

"Good," he whispered, "good. So, no longer a diamond in the rough with such glorious wings as those."

Freya nodded and the wings fluttered. "Yes, they're beautiful," she said. "Soon I will perhaps get a pair of my very own."

"I will lend you mine, brave girl," said Morton. "If you use them well," he added, "perhaps I will give them to you. It seems already you have used them well. It seems to me you used them well before you even got them, for you have this day been a girl of winged feet and winged words and winged spirit. It's only natural that you should have them. For my part, I have a feeling I won't have need of them when I fly out of here tonight."

"Tush," said Freya. "Tush," and the tears were streaming down her cheeks. "Don't say such things. Of course you will have need of them."

"I have been contemplating the saga of my life," said Morton. He could see that all the people in the field still stood silently listening, and wondered to himself what kind of sounds they heard when he spoke. It's true that although the people gathered here could not possibly have understood a word he said, they sensed somehow that cradled here in the arms of this young Valkyrie was the central figure in all of Norway, on this day at least.

"Cradled here in this, the warmest home I've ever had, I have been reflecting upon the vistas I have seen, the kings I have encountered, and those few I've met — those very, very few — who, like you, have been truly brave. The thought that I will be remembered by someone so young and bold, the thought that my flight will live on in the strength of your arms, the thought that I have had the honour of giving such a gift—these are the great legacies of my life, though I had no inkling of them before yesterday. These are the thoughts that allow me to take leave of this life with a full heart."

Freya was truly weeping now. "Don't say such things," she cried. "You said to me that a Valkyrie was a chooser of the slain. If that's true, then it may not be in my power to choose you to live, but I will not choose you to die!"

"It is not for you to choose," he whispered, but she did not heed him and went on.

"And if I can choose that you do not die, then that is what I choose, for if I am anyone's Valkyrie, dear Morton, then I am yours."

"Are you indeed?" asked Morton, and his eyes flashed in a moment of one golden thought. "If you choose to be my Valkyrie, then will you take me to Odin's hall?"

"One day I will," said Freya softly. "One day, after you have lived a long and full life of freedom, and you and I have flown many times together to see the sun. Then, when it is time for you to go, I will carry you myself to Odin's Hall. Wherever it is, even if it is beyond the boundless sea, I will carry you there. Even if I cannot find it, even if it's not to be found, I will carry you there. And then you shall find yourself a place amongst the greatest, the wisest, the most valiant

Viking warriors that ever lived, and I will bring you the drinking horn of victory."

"And you, my girl," whispered Morton, his eyes closing again around the pleasure of this thought, "you shall be the last of the Valkyries, and the greatest of them all. Fly well, my girl, for they will still remember and speak your name ten centuries from now."

"And yours too, my falcon," said the weeping Freya, "and yours too. But not yet. So I say to you: Do not die!"

But Morton had chosen this moment to take his leave from the battlefield of northern Norway. He lay very still in her arms, his body as weightless there as a clutch of dry leaves, for it is a well-known fact about free birds of any kind: their spirits outweigh the rest of their bodies, and Morton was a free bird despite his lifetime of servitude.

Freya buried her face in the bird's neck and wept and wept and wept, and her wings enclosed around them both and shivered as she wept. And her tears fell in golden drops to the ground, and where they touched the roots of trees beneath the snow they turned, in their own quiet way, to amber.

For a long time the Norsemen and women stood, silently regarding the enclosed pair that seemed for all the world to be joined as one, and a sadness gripped their hearts that made them long for their homes and the living arms of those they loved. Rolf stepped forward and tucked a great hand underneath the weeping girl's wing, laid it gently upon her shoulder and held it there for a long time, surrounded by a king and the people of a reunited Norway.

And The Beaky stood there too, and watched and waited in sadness and respect with all the rest, and he considered to himself how a king without his people is like a bird without his feathers. If a king cultivates the life of his people, then everyone in the land will be as a feather to beautify the plumage of the king. The sight of that girl and her bird was enough to make The Beaky believe that all the strife and violence and struggle had faded from the earth in the instant of their embrace. But he knew better. The life he had once led made him know better. As long as there was shame and fear mixed with the desire for a better life in the world, there would be strife, he thought, and trouble on our poor earth. But enough of this unschooled Beaky philosophy. I make my run to the end of my tale.

20

Return

THE OLD MAN is sitting in his chair and reading from his favourite books by the light of a nearby candle. He tries not to worry, for his children know the forest like the back of their hands and sometimes in their wandering they forget the time of day and come home late. It's true he believes that they have only been missing for one day when in fact they have been missing for two, but we must forgive him for that. He is finally realizing that he has been neglecting them lately. More, he knows he has been dwelling too much on the past: shadow wars and secret battles that once were fought in a place far away from here, outside the human realm. Again, we must forgive him for this, since he lost there the only woman he had ever loved. He believed then that she would one day return, but she did not. And so, with time, his burden has grown heavier.

He knows as well that lately he has very nearly broken the solemn oath he once swore to never speak of these things. He recalls his recent weakness and is ashamed. Still, if you could see his face right now, you would know that a change has come over him. He has been gripped with a new resolve. "I must be strong," he says to himself. "For my children. I must find a way."

He lays his book down and looks at the door. After another moment he rises, pulls his coat from the wall and walks toward it. As he reaches to grasp the handle the red painted door comes open by itself, and his daughter is there, standing in the doorway, a world of darkness behind her, looking up into his face. He sees in an instant everything that is new and old about her, the weight of sadness in her face that hovers there in the shadow and light of the little candle behind him. He sees the wings that are folded neatly along her back and his face flushes now into a long banished colour of youth. He takes a step back as she comes inside and moves further into the light, and in the next moment her brother is there, leaning with his head through the doorway and looking from his sister to his father and back again, waiting for her to speak. When the words finally come they are not surprising, neither to him nor to the father who has waited for this moment for many years, wondering when and whether it would ever come.

"Tell me about my mother," she says.

Acknowledgements

In preparation for this book, I read *From the Sagas of the Norse Kings* — a beautiful translation and edit of *Snorri Sturluson's Heimskringla* by Erling Monsen.

Thanks to Carl Wilson for reading an early draft of this novel; Amy Black and Linda Pruessen for providing spectacular notes; Kent Dixon for suggesting it become a trilogy; Laura Fernandez, Gillian Burnett, Ann-Marie MacDonald, Michael Redhill and Hilary McMahon, for pushing me down the long road towards publication; David Petersen, for donning the real feathered cloak, and Estelle Shook, of the Caravan Farm Theatre in the Okanagan Valley of B.C., for inspiring the play upon which this novel is based.